My Best Friend's Brother

Laura Ellen Kennedy

Piccadilly Press • London

To Andrew and Ellie Nelson, for inspiration
With thanks to Celia, CosmoGIRL!
team members and readers

First published in Great Britain in 2007
by Piccadilly Press Ltd,
5 Castle Road, London NW1 8PR
www.piccadillypress.co.uk

A catalogue record for this book is available from the British Library

ISBN-13:978 1 85340 922 6 (trade paperback)

1 3 5 7 9 10 8 6 4 2

Printed in the UK by CPI Bookmarque, Croydon, CR0 4TD
Typeset by Textype, Cambridge, based on a design by Louise Millar
Cover design by Sue Hellard and Simon Davis
Set in StempelGaramond and Carumba

Chapter 1

♥

It was the night of the Hallowe'en dance last year and the hall looked amazing. Silver light from the chandeliers glittered off the mirrors and soaked into soft red velvet curtains. Gold-painted chairs and tables completed the illusion of grandeur. After weeks of work and organising, it was the best feeling to see it all finished. Watching the looks on everyone's faces as the function hall at the Broadwick Hotel gradually filled up, I thought I might burst with pride.

I'd been on the event committee and we'd all agreed we wanted to steer clear of all the traditional witches, pumpkins and broomsticks. OK, I'll admit it was probably out of vanity more than wanting to be creative and original – but we hardly wanted to be dressed up as mummies and vampires and lose out on the chance to look glamorous, let alone see all the guys in their tuxes. So we eventually decided on a gothic castle theme. And, not to brag or anything, but we'd done brilliantly with just the money we'd scraped together through ticket sales and fund-raisers.

I'd managed to bribe quite a few of the other art students at college with free tickets and they'd done an amazing job glitzing up the furniture and sculpting fake stone gargoyles and archways. I thought of all those hours we'd spent on the phone, begging and borrowing from local firms and persuading students' friends and relatives to help out – and knew it had been worth it.

Dashing home from helping set everything up that afternoon, so I could get ready before the limo was due, had been a rush, but I was running on excitement. When I arrived back at the hall with my best friend, Sally, her date, Mark, and her brother, Jake, I'd honestly felt like an A-lister arriving at the Oscars – setting the red carpet up outside had been a genius touch.

'Erica, it looks amazing!' Sally gasped as we walked in. She gave me a little hug and added quietly, 'And you look beautiful.' She grabbed my hand. 'We are going to have the *best* night. Come on, let's go and see if we can get the music cranked up – I want to get everyone dancing.'

I couldn't stop grinning. I don't think I'd ever felt happier.

Being the centre of attention wasn't something that happened to me. Neither was feeling pretty, not like I did that night. I had my small group of close friends at college, but at school I was the one who blended into the background – the small, pale, freckly girl people would never remember. Don't get me wrong, I didn't spend my life wishing I was someone else. Going unnoticed can work in your favour sometimes – and all the really popular girls seemed to have to work so hard to please everyone. Besides, if I ever felt hard done by, Mum would go off on a rant, saying I had two arms and legs that worked, I was bright and had a loving family and plenty to be grateful for and that I was luckier than an awful lot of people in the world.

But all the boys loved Sally. Actually, *everyone* loved Sally. And she could look glamorous in anything. She has this long mane of glossy, dark hair. (She swore to me there was no secret to it, but I still made her write a list for me once, of all the shampoos, conditioners and styling products she used, so I could try them one by one, looking for a miracle. But I guess she was just born lucky.) Her clear, olive skin, her womanly curves and beautiful, dark eyes meant people noticed her. Most infuriatingly, she was also the loveliest person I knew. If she'd ever acted like she thought she was perfect or knew the power she had over people, I might have begrudged her, but she had as many days as I did where she looked in the mirror and turned up her nose at what she saw. In a way it made me feel better when she confided in me that she hated her nose or she thought her knees looked podgy – if someone as perfect

3

as her could still find fault with her looks, maybe my own flaws weren't as bad as I imagined. When I longed to be taller or stared hatefully at my pale, un-tan-able complexion, I'd remind myself even Sally thought things like that, and it helped me stop worrying.

For once, though, that night, I didn't feel like the plain-best-friend. I felt like some of the people looking in our direction might actually be looking at me. I'd coloured my hair darker and piled it up in a mess of curls. In the gothic spirit, I'd brushed on as much dark, silver-grey eye shadow as I dared. And I absolutely loved my dress. I had my big sister Tamara to thank for that. I'd gone to stay with her, a few weeks before the dance, in her shared university house in Newcastle.

We'd spent a lovely Saturday wandering around town, shopping and sitting in cafés, and we found this antiquey-looking burgundy dress in a vintage shop. I loved it, but it was at least a size too big. Despite my protests, Tamara still made me try it on. She said it was the perfect colour for me and just wanted to see what it would look like. In the changing room it was heartbreaking to see how lovely it would have been if it hadn't hung off me like some sort of comedy clown suit. For a minute I almost wondered if it might be worth putting on a stone just to fill it out.

I was thinking of all the Green and Blacks I could eat to help when Tamara said she was going to buy it for me. For a minute I thought she'd read my mind and was about to protest I didn't really want to gain a stone, when I realised mind-reading doesn't actually happen. I crumpled my face at her, not understanding. I said I'd never wear it. But she launched into this speech, saying people made this mistake way too often, forgetting you can get clothes altered. She's so bossy.

'How often do you find a dress you love as much as this? You'll look amazing in it – we just have to take it to a dressmaker and get it taken in, that's all. It won't be all that expensive and we'll probably still end up paying less than you would for a new one as nice.' So she paid and then took me to a tailor and they pinned the dress. We left it there and a week or so later Tamara sent it to me in the post. She was so right. When I put it on I felt like a different person. In fact, I was so inspired by the transformation it sparked a new passion: I asked Mum to get her old sewing machine down from the loft, along with all her dressmaking books and patterns, and she taught me some of the basics. I revived loads of my old clothes, customising forgotten T-shirts and adding my own twists.

Anyway, I'm going off the subject (being 'tangential' as

my dad always says while he moans at me for 'lacking focus'). But my point is: the Hallowe'en dance was the first chance I'd had to wear my 'magic' dress. And maybe it swelled my ego just a bit too much, but I thought I'd seen a look in Jake's eyes, when we'd all piled into the limo, that I hadn't seen before. When he said I looked great, I let myself believe he wasn't just being his gentlemanly, lovely self. I thought, just maybe, possibly, he was seeing a new side to me. I was even his 'date'. Sort of. Technically. Well, only because Sally wanted to bring her boyfriend *and* her brother – and I'd given up on having anyone actually officially ask me to the dance long before – so when Sally asked if Jake could be my totally-just-friends-plus-one, while a little part of me was hurt that she'd obviously given up hope on me getting a date too, actually, secretly, if I could have chosen anyone to go with it would have been Jake, so it worked out almost perfectly – and I said of course.

I was in such a euphoric mood, I let all these little scenarios play over and over in my mind – like a montage from some cheesy film – me and Jake giggling together over the punch bowl, Jake complimenting my event-organising prowess and being irresistibly drawn to me because of my talents, me and Jake dancing a slow dance together, staring into each other's eyes . . .

As the evening got going, though, I was happily distracted. We had so much fun dancing and chatting to everyone. It was really packed out – as it turned out, probably a little too packed out. Jimmy Burton, who did law with Sally and had a reputation as a troublemaker, had turned up, obviously from the pub, with a gang of his older footie mates. They were being rowdy and messing about, picking on this guy – I recognised him from around college but I wasn't sure of his name, it might have been David. Jimmy had obviously got hold of the guy's wallet somehow and was rifling through it, waving his personal things about and taunting him. Jimmy's chunky, strawberry-blond frame was shaking with chuckles of amusement, and the sound of his laugh carried across the room despite the loud music.

When maybe-David tried to snatch the wallet back, Jimmy just laughed at first, but was then clearly unimpressed when he came close to actually getting hold of it and reclaiming it. So Jimmy decided to start a game of catch. Some of his mates spread out, ready to field the game. Jimmy's closest crony, Alex, was barging backward towards the end of the buffet table, near where Sally was standing close to the punch, chatting with our friend Ruth, and I started to get a creeping feeling in my stomach. As I hurried over, Jimmy sent this wallet flying towards Alex, but powerful as his throw was, it wasn't on target. It was heading straight for the back of Sally's head just as she was sipping punch from a delicate champagne flute (it was only a plastic champagne flute, but it was the sort of thin, tough plastic that could easily crack and cut you just like glass).

It was weird, but I could almost see it all unfolding in my mind, as if in slow motion: the wallet hitting Sally, her face slamming forward into her drink, breaking that brittle plastic into sharp shards which pierced her skin and sent blood running down her chin. Without thinking too much, I sprang into action. Urgh, I still cringe when I think about it but, on instinct, I dived behind her, like some crazed goalie, into the trajectory of the wallet, and my hand made contact! Having always been pretty rubbish at contact sports, there was a fraction of a second then, when I felt very pleased with myself. I watched with relief as the wallet headed off safely towards Alex's face, and wondered if I'd missed a calling to football stardom.

But I hadn't exactly planned what would happen next. I couldn't stop myself falling in time to avoid smashing into the sharp corner of buffet table. We'd had to do things as cheaply as we could, and the tables weren't the sturdiest, so, of course, the entire thing collapsed under me. There was a monumental crash as plates of food and bowls of punch came down on me. I felt a searing pain, first in my side as I hit the table, then in my arm as I landed on it. And there'd been a horrible ripping sound. I tried desperately not to acknowledge that it could have been my dress coming to an untimely end.

It was truly mortifying. The chatter stopped as everyone spun round to look at me then quickly erupted into laughter and shouting. A whole room of people laughing at me. I'm sure I did look funny but I wasn't seeing the humorous side. I was in shock and I'm not sure I could have moved if Sally and Ruth hadn't come straight to my rescue, deftly helping me up and ushering me out of the hall.

I wasn't badly injured but my arm was bleeding a bit and it hurt. I was shaking. There was food and drink all over me, in my hair, on my face and all down my left side; and I had this heartbreaking sensation of air blowing on to my right side, through my lovely dress. I knew it was torn. I could still hear the commotion in the hall and I burst into tears. Sally, bless her, whisked me into the ladies.

'Those guys are such a waste of space!' she growled. 'Don't worry, hon, that cut'll wash up easily – it's not serious. I don't think any of that food will stain, either.'

I sobbed as she pulled wads of paper towels out of the dispenser and filled a sink with water. As she dabbed at me, my head was filled with nightmare flashbacks of all those laughing faces. I stared at my bedraggled reflection and raised my arm to look at the damage to my dress.

'Oh, Erica!' Sally realised what had happened and peered carefully at the fabric. 'Ah, don't worry, it'll fix! It's lucky, it's along the seam – you can sew that up and you'll hardly see it. I bet I can even sort it out pretty neatly for now with some safety pins. Hold on, you keep washing yourself up and I'll go in search of safety-pins and make-up bags!' She reached up gingerly and touched the sticky, matted mess that had been my hair, then she looked me in the eyes and smiled. 'Don't you worry, we'll get you sorted out in ten minutes, I promise.' And with a squeeze of my arm she whirled out of the door.

I loved Sally then, always calm in a crisis, with a soothing power only my mum could equal. But there was no consoling me. I dabbed pathetically at my dress for a few moments. As I squeezed the paper towel into the sink, it was like watching all my dreams swirl dirtily down the plughole. I looked into the mirror and the ridiculousness of it all welled up in me. I honestly didn't know if I was going to laugh or cry and what came out was a sort of strangled mixture of both.

Even though I'd barely had a chance to speak to Jake all night, suddenly going back to the party was the last thing I wanted. The loud pounding of the music on the other side of the wall felt alien and oppressive. I needed to escape. So I took all the pins out of my hair, rinsed it deeply under the tap and scraped it back into a bun. Then I swung open the door into the lobby, hurriedly fetched my coat from the cloakroom and rushed out into the night air. There was a bench under a tree just on the right of the hotel forecourt and I claimed it, wrapping my coat tightly round me and hugging my knees. To think, less than two hours before, I'd stepped out of that car with all those expectations and then there I was, sticky and soaked and alone. I stared up at the starry sky and sacrificed what was left of my mascara to more sobs of self-pity.

Chapter 2

♥

I f you've ever found yourself looking at a friend you've known forever and suddenly seen them, I mean really seen them, as if it was the first time – as if they were a stranger again and you were rediscovering all the shapes of their features like new treasures – if that's happened to you, you might understand what I felt the day I fell for Jake.

I'd known Jake and Sally since I was eight, from when they moved into our street. Tamara and I knocked on their door and introduced ourselves with that too-young-to-know-better brazenness that kids have. From that day on, we'd all hang out together: me, Sally, Jake – who's just a year and a half older than me and Sal – and Tam for a while, before she went off to uni. I have all these summer memories of running about in our front gardens playing ball games, or hide and seek behind the dustbins and garages.

Sally and I were soon best friends. We started secondary school together, sat next to each other on the bus every day, and in the evenings we'd turn up on each other's doorsteps after dinner and hang out in her room or my garden, depending on the time of year. She was the first person I went to when I was excited about something or needed a whinge or a cry. We got to be like sisters, only we were closer than I ever was to Tamara, because we were the same age and went through everything together.

The evening everything changed was a late-August evening, after seven p.m. I guess, because the light was beginning to turn from evening amber to that inky, dusk colour. Sally and I were lying on a blanket on my front lawn, staring up into the sky talking. We'd gabble constantly, about anything from which was the best chocolate biscuit, to all our deepest philosophies on life. Mum would say she couldn't understand how we still found stuff to talk about, when we practically spent every waking minute together. But somehow we always had as many things to discuss as there are atoms in the air.

Sally had a crush on this boy called Mark, and we were giggling about how she was going to trick him into asking her out when Jake's face appeared in the air above us.

'What are you up to, ladies?' he asked.

'Right now? Getting a better view up your nose than I

13

ever wanted,' I said, and his hand shot up to cover his nose.

'Well sit up then, and stop lying about like . . . layabouts!' he half shouted and half laughed, and I kicked myself for letting my mouth run off on its own again before my brain had a chance to stop it.

'Sorry . . .' Sally and I dragged ourselves into sitting positions as Jake joined us on the blanket. 'I was just joking you know, your nose is great, er, I mean it's fine, you know . . .' I was no smooth-talker.

Sally tried to rescue me. 'Erica! Shhhhh. Don't stress out so much!' She made a cross-eyed face at me, then turned and started chatting to Jake about some family business or other while I looked down and waited for my red face to fade. What a doofus.

As I glanced back up, Jake laughed at something Sally was saying and this incredible grin flashed across his face. As I watched, the power of it rushed through me and sort of spun me. I don't know how it was possible when I knew him so well, but, as his dark eyes sparkled, my heart skipped. I couldn't tear my gaze away, so I just stared. It was like I was drinking him in. His dark hair was damp because he'd just come back from swimming, and it was getting a bit long, so it curled at the ends and licked at his face and neck.

I was sort of paralysed and hot and spinning at the same time. My heart was racing loudly, but it was like the sound outside me was muted and all I could see was Jake. This new Jake, who had somehow changed from being a big, familiar kid to a nineteen-year-old man in a split second right in front of me. I couldn't help looking at his broad, toned shoulders as he leaned forward, legs crossed, resting his elbows on his knees. He was fiddling with a tuft of grass he'd torn from the ground, and even his hands and wrists were suddenly overwhelmingly gorgeous.

I was properly confused. I'd slipped into some parallel universe where everything was altered – why hadn't anyone else noticed? What was happening? I was terrified that this urge to reach out and touch him would override my brain and my arm would shoot out and grab hold of him before I could stop it.

'Are you OK?' Suddenly I realised Sally was watching me – I was probably goggling like some total idiot. The spell was broken, but I felt as if I'd had an electric shock or something.

'Umm, oh yes,' I mumbled. 'I mean, no, I feel a bit weird suddenly. Er, stay there, I'm just going to get a glass of water. Or something with a lot of sugar in it, or caffeine, or something.' I levered myself to my feet and headed towards the door before I remembered my manners and spun back round. 'Oh, do you guys want drinks?'

But I don't think I listened to their answers. I was kind of terrified, or excited, or just weirded out. Things had changed all at once and I wasn't sure if it was temporary – it didn't feel it. I still can't explain what happened in that instant, but I remember not being able to sleep that night (or for a few nights after that, actually) because I was thinking about Jake. Every time I closed my eyes, I saw him smiling and laughing and being utterly gorgeous – in a totally sneaky crept-up-on-me way, I have to say. Then I'd think about when I'd see him next and it made me smile uncontrollably. But then I'd think of Sally and imagine how grossed out she'd be if she knew what I was thinking, and that made me feel like some sort of pervert. Then the thought of Jake knowing what I was thinking was even more mortifying. He probably thought of me as another little sister. We were practically family, after all – my mum and Sally's mum both said Sally and I might as well be sisters. Oh God. I think I eventually exhausted myself to sleep imagining how hard it was going to be, keeping this secret.

Well, I'd kept it for the longest, most agonising two months of my life. Each day at college, when we'd hang out with our male friends and they were so immature, I'd be comparing them to Jake. Some of the best-looking ones were the worst – they treated girls like rubbish because they knew they could get away with it. Most of the others were just sort of goofy and idiotic. They made me think of puppies, getting over-excited and running into walls or falling over – only not in a cute way. It just confirmed all the things that made Jake different. He never seemed to need to be loud to impress anyone. He was strong, but not macho and idiotic about it like the stupid guys who deliberately got into fights or did dumb stunts to prove how hard they were or how much pain they could handle.

Each time I'd see him, he'd look a little bit more gorgeous than he had the time before, and, every time he was sweet or gentle or polite, I'd think how it was so amazing the way he didn't worry that being nice would make him seem weak, like every other guy seemed to think.

I'd fallen in love with him a little more each day. But as I sat on that bench outside the Broadwick Hotel in semi-darkness, for the first time in those long weeks, I realised what a naive idiot I'd been, holding on to the hope that he might actually come to like me. After that night I was going to be a laughing stock. I covered my face with my hands as the sight of that food avalanche coming down on me flashed through my head again, with the sounds of the shouting and jeering. Thank goodness there was only a couple of terms of college left.

I was just starting to plan how I could get to classes whilst minimising the risk of being seen or spoken to, when I heard someone call my name. I scrunched myself tighter into a ball and stayed quiet. If I closed my eyes hard enough maybe I could just disappear. But then, there was Jake.

'There you are, we've all been looking for you! Sal's frantic.'

I didn't answer, I felt so tired. I put a self-conscious hand up to my bedraggled, scraped-back hair and Jake sat down beside me. When he looked at me his voice softened. 'You're crying. You're not worried about that lot in there, are you? They're having a great time, they've forgotten already . . . Come back inside.' He was being so sweet, as ever, but I couldn't tell him what was really wrong, why I felt so sorry for myself.

'I don't think I can. I'm not worried what people think,' I lied, 'or even that I look a mess. Things didn't exactly turn out as I'd planned tonight.' I tried my hardest to sound jokey. 'But it's fine. I'm just kind of . . . done, you know?' I thought again of how I'd seen the evening in my mind, through a sort of Vaseline-coated lens, me looking like a movie star, dancing with Jake, gazing into his eyes . . . Of *course* things didn't turn out how I'd planned! What a stupid little girl. I couldn't stop myself blubbing again and, when Jake put his hand on my shoulder, this incredible shiver ran through me.

I glanced up at him. He looked amazing in his tux and his face just turned me to jelly. His strong jaw and nose, his soft lips, and his beautiful, gentle eyes, looking at me all concerned and caring, all made me lose my senses for a moment.

'Jake I . . . ' I couldn't believe I was going to tell him, but I knew the words were about to spill out. 'I wanted us to dance together. This stupid dress . . . I wanted you to see me as *me*, not just your little sister's geeky friend. But it all went wrong and here I am looking like a hideous mess and you probably hate me for running out on Sal without telling her . . . '

I looked down at my feet, embarrassed, realising I was going to regret this outburst later. But then Jake reached out and gently touched my face. His fingers curled into a little cradle under my chin, and he turned my head to face him. I thought I might faint. When I looked at his face, his expression wasn't full of pity like I'd expected, his eyes were shining and he was smiling at me.

'Erica, you're not a mess. You look beautiful. You always look beautiful. In fact, weirdly, you're more beautiful than ever right now because your messed-up hair and your streaky face all show you're a loyal friend and you'll always be there for Sal when she needs you. You were worried she was going to get hurt and you stepped in to protect her. That's more important than perfect hair and a lovely dress.' He paused for a second and I think my heart stopped beating too.

'And, I haven't thought of you as just Sal's friend since we were like, fourteen. I was always kind of hoping *you* might think of *me* as more than just Sal's brother . . . ' He was half laughing as I tried to get my head round what he was saying. All this time – he'd been waiting for *me* to notice *him*? I couldn't believe it. I didn't want to move or say anything, in case it turned out I'd misheard, or he'd been joking.

I reached up, shaking, to touch his hand, which was still cupping my chin, and our fingers touched. I closed my eyes for a second as he brought his other hand up to my face too. He held my head so softly in his grasp and with his thumbs brushed away what was left of my tears. My skin was dancing. As he moved closer it all felt so unreal, it almost seemed like I was outside my body looking down at myself. He leaned in towards me and his lips just brushed mine. My whole body tingled till I couldn't feel my feet. He softly kissed my cheek, then the other, and then his fingertips stroked down my neck and, slowly, he found my lips again and we kissed. As the cold breeze teased around us, our lips were hot and Jake's kisses were light and then passionate. I was in a new world.

Chapter 3

M y eyes opened and pinstripes of morning sunlight decorated my bedroom wall through the blinds. Everything seemed the same but I was different. For a split second I imagined the whole of the night before had been a dream. But there was my dress, tattered and torn and blotched with half-mopped food stains, and there was Jake's jacket draped over the hanger.

He'd tried one more time to persuade me to go back in to the dance and, when I'd refused (who could care about a boring dance after a kiss like that?), he texted Sal to let her know I was OK and we walked up to the station to get a cab home. I'd been cold in the taxi, even with my jacket on, and Jake put his round me too. We held hands the whole way home, and I couldn't help staring at our intertwined fingers to reassure myself it was real. Every time I looked round at him, he'd be smiling at me. We paid the driver and Jake had walked me to my door and we'd kissed good-night, the most amazing kiss good-night.

I opened the blinds and stared out into the crisp, autumnal brightness, then jumped back into bed and snuggled up in my duvet, grinning with deep contentment as I remembered my last glimpse of Jake, smiling at me as I'd closed the door.

My phone beeped and I leaped to pick it up and read the text.

Are you free to come over? Nice day for a walk . . . Jxx.

He'd read my mind. I'd got half a word into my reply when there was another bleep.

Hey hon, hope ur ok. Didn't miss much after you left + don't worry, everyone forgot about the incident. Hot choc in town in a bit?

I felt suddenly guilt-ridden. I'd been about to arrange to see Jake, without a thought of turning up on his doorstep like I'd done twenty million times before – only this time I'd be there to see Jake, not Sally. I realised I might not be that impressed if the shoe were on the other foot. Oh God. Like Chandler says in *The One Where Joey Moves Out*: Can: open. Worms: everywhere.

What if Sally didn't approve, or was freaked out? She was the most important person in my life – we'd always been there for each other – but I'd been so swept up in the moment the night before, I hadn't even thought about what my getting together with Jake could mean for

Sally. If things didn't work out with Jake, she'd be angry with me, or angry with him. Even if neither of us did anything wrong, if we split up, there'd be all this awkwardness, I wouldn't be able to go over to hers any more, maybe she wouldn't want to come to mine either or even be friends any more . . . As I got more and more stressed, I realised I had to sort this out right away, so I texted Jake back.

Just made a date with Sal, u free early evening, 5ish?'

Jake replied that was cool and he'd come and knock for me, so I replied to Sally: *Genius plan, need to shower, see you outside in 40 mins?*

I was nervous: it was so odd. I was doing the simplest thing I'd done a million times, meeting Sally and driving into town for a drink, and I felt nervous. Outside, Sally was waiting in the car, nodding her head to her terrible dance music, and as she saw me coming she grinned and gave me a cheesy thumbs up. I couldn't help grinning back. I flopped into the passenger seat and slammed the door.

'Hold on to your seatbelt, babe, it's full speed to Coco's for a morning-after, full-fat latte with chocolate syrup!' And with a deft but slightly-too-fast reverse turn, we were off.

We parked by the market square and were walking to the cashpoint when Sally broke the silence.

'You seem quiet; you're not worried about last night, are you? I know it was horrible the way everyone was laughing, but it was knee-jerk, you know. Once the stuff was tidied, everyone was either asking after you, worried if you were OK, or had honestly forgotten about it. Well, everyone except Jo Davy, who was stirring a bit, but then she's just an eternal cow anyway and everyone knows it. We had a really cool time until it happened – try to remember that bit. It wasn't so much fun after you left anyway.'

Bless Sally for bending the truth in the sweetest way to try and make me feel better.

'Oh my God, it was mortifying. I'm sure I'm going to be known as "the-weirdo-girl-who-launched-herself-at-the-buffet-at-the-Hallowe'en-ball" for the rest of my college career. But to hell with it, I can laugh at myself. Anyway, if it gets too bad I can just emigrate. They probably haven't heard about it in Australia yet.' We laughed and linked arms as we walked the last few yards to Coco's.

Coco's is the best little coffee and cake shop in town, and probably the best I've been to anywhere, ever. It's in the more hidden, winding part of town, near the church, and it's shamelessly sweet-toothed – I don't think you can get so much as a cheese sandwich for savoury snacks, but there are freshly baked cakes and biscuits and pastries, and a bigger array of syrups, sauces and spreads than I've seen in any of the big chain coffee places. We pulled open the door and walked up to the counter, enveloped in warm, sweet, milky-smelling air. There was a gentle murmur of chat bubbling under the frothy whirr of the coffee machine.

We were soon sitting down with our drinks and a slab of toffee apple cake to share, and I felt guilty about doing a runner on Sally the night before.

'I'm sorry I didn't come back to the dance last night. Thanks for trying to sort me out, you were great, but I just couldn't face it. I knew I'd need a few hours to relocate my sense of humour, by which time it would have been over anyway . . . '

Sally looked genuinely surprised. 'No, no, don't be silly, I totally get it. Totally. I just feel bad that your night ended the way it did after the work you put into making it such a great time for everyone else'.

'Well, actually . . . ' I felt my face burning pink as I said it, 'it didn't turn out to be such a bad night after all.' I couldn't stifle my smile, and Sally's eyebrows shot up mid sip. Taking care not to choke, she put her drink down with a business-like resolution and a quizzical smile that told me I was going nowhere until I'd explained myself fully. This was it, then. No going back.

'Erica Mitford, spill it, right now. What did you do?! Jake texted me to say he was going to bring you right home in a cab. Did you change your mind and go out somewhere?'

'No, no, he did bring me straight home really, it's not like we went out or anything. We walked and talked and stuff, and Jake was really sweet and made me feel better and it was just . . . nice. A really nice end to the evening after all.' I had a lump in my throat thinking about it, I was so happy, and I couldn't suppress my blushes even though I was genuinely worried Sally might not be pleased. I couldn't look her in the face.

'I don't get it, do you mean . . .?' Sally was trying to make sense of my burbling. 'Erica.' She leaned forward to read my face and I looked up, still flushed and nervous. 'You and Jake?'

I couldn't speak. I just nodded and felt so overwhelmed, I had to swallow some tears. What a wuss! But I had to pull myself together; I owed her that.

'Sally, I think he likes me too, we sort of . . . got together – I think.' I shrugged, as if that made it less huge. 'But listen,' I looked her in the eyes and was serious, 'if it's going to be weird for you, we don't have to be . . . I mean I don't want to do anything to complicate things, it's really important to me. I don't even know if it really means anything, it was just a few kisses – argh, I feel so weird telling you!' I clamped my face in my hands and through my fingers searched Sally's stunned expression, which slowly broke into a broad smile and she let out a squeal.

'Erica!' She reached across the table and punched me on the shoulder. 'That's brilliant!'

I didn't want to believe I'd heard right.

'I mean it!' she said. 'I always thought there might be something between you two, but you're both so stubborn and secretive . . . but I think it's great, really. And you worry too much. It'll be fine! We all hang out together anyway, we'll be fine.' She thought for a second and squealed again. 'We can do double dates! It's going to be so much fun!' She grabbed my hands and shook them about in excitement like a little kid. I was so relieved. Then she grimaced. 'I don't know what you wanted to *kiss* him for though, bleugh.' She stuck her tongue out and mimicked sticking her finger down her throat. 'Gross.'

chapter 4

♥

I was checking the mirror and fiddling with my hair for about the fiftieth time when Jake knocked on the door. My heart was flapping manically like a fish out of water. I ran down the stairs and practically smacked into the front door I was in such a hurry. Smooth.

Jake grinned at me with raised eyebrows as I opened the door.

'I probably would have waited, you know,' he said, 'even if it had taken you, say, a whole minute to get to the door.'

'Shut it.' I blushed and turned towards the kitchen. Mum and Dad were at the table chatting, glasses of wine in hand, amid the warm food smells and pans bubbling on the stove. Mum leaned and peered.

'Well! Hello, Jake.' She started to look worryingly like she might get up, so I hurried through the door, practically knocking Jake off the doorstep.

'Just going for a quick walk, back in a bit!' I called, and shut the door before she could get nosy. She can move pretty fast when she wants gossip.

At the end of the driveway, Jake put his arm round me and pulled me tightly to him. A warm rush ran through me like a head-to-toe smile. I put my arm round his waist and we walked like that, holding on to each other. I looked up at him and he looked back and leaned down and kissed me. It's quite tricky walking like that, though, and the kiss soon dissolved into giggles as we veered dangerously close to a lamppost. It was weird how natural it felt after all the years of being friends, being more. And in the light of day – well, dusk – it felt real. The night before hadn't just been a moment of madness.

'How was Coco's?' Jake asked.

'Good thanks . . .' My nerves returned then, knowing Sally must have mentioned where we were going, because I hadn't. 'Did you see Sally when she got in?'

'Yup. She punched me. She said if I wasn't nice to you she'd strangle me quietly in my sleep.'

'Ha! Cheeky mare!' I giggled. But I couldn't shake my worry. 'She seemed all right though, didn't she? It was such a relief when she seemed happy . . . you know . . . but she's my absolute best friend, well you know that. I'm just so scared things are going to get complicated . . . ' I was burbling.

Jake turned me to face him. We'd reached the gate of the footpath that led through the churchyard, and we were tucked away from the road, standing in the shelter of a little Tudor cottage.

'You worry too much, Erica. Nothing's going to go wrong. I'd never do anything to hurt you, you know.'

'I know,' I said. His sweetness soothed me a little, but I knew deep inside you just can't make promises like that. No one can know what the future holds and people do things all the time to hurt people they love, not deliberately but just because you can't help it sometimes. But Jake rested his hand tenderly in the crook of my neck, his fingers playing in my hair. We kissed again, and I knew he was right. What was the point of worrying about something that hasn't happened?

We walked through the churchyard and up on to the hill, sat on the slightly damp grass and watched the night fall. Somehow I didn't feel the cold. I felt safe and happy and warm as we talked and held hands.

It was nearly eight by the time we got back to our street. I didn't want to let go of him and we just stood for a while, holding on to each other as we talked. He had work the next day. He was taking a year out before university and was working as many shifts as he could in the picture framing and art shop in town to earn cash. But we agreed to meet up in town when he finished at four p.m.

From then on, we saw each other every day, and it was like I had a new home. There was nowhere I felt safer than with Jake. Sometimes I couldn't get my head round how I'd lived my life before, in some sort of black-and-white half-life. Well, I could go on and on about how amazing it was, but basically I'd turned into some soppy girly-girl. And I was loving it too much to be disgusted with myself.

On Bonfire Night, Sally and Mark and Jake and I went to a family fireworks display at the local primary school. I'd had my doubts about the plan – my mum and maybe my dad would be there, and loads of little kids, and their grandparents probably. It wasn't exactly cool. But it turned out to be fun. Mark drove into the village at Sally's command and we did the double-date thing. Sally and Mark bickered jokingly and rolled their eyes a lot at each other while Jake and I quietly held hands as we laughed and chatted with them. At the school there were hot dogs and squares of warm ginger cake. There were marsh-mallows on sticks you could toast on the bonfire, and really good hot chocolate.

We found a spot to settle against the back wall of the school hall, which faced out on to the field so we had a good view of the fireworks. We all huddled together and the colour-filled, popping and fizzing explosions began.

My pink-gloved hands were clamped cosily around my hot chocolate, but the best feeling was just being there, happily squashed between my best friend and my boyfriend. (Boyfriend! Ha! I was still feeling the disbelieving joy of using the phrase 'my boyfriend'. Even if it was just in my head and I hadn't actually said it out loud to anyone yet, especially Jake!)

I suppose you could say I was a late starter. I'd been out with a couple of boys before GCSEs, but I don't think either lasted more than a week. The first boy, James, was some sort of crazed notch-maker – he got his hands on any girl he could, any time he could. No rules applied. The second boy, Anthony, I'd actually fancied, but it turned out he saw me as little more than a stepping stone, a hand to hold while he worked up the courage to ask out the girl he really liked. Sally. Of course, she sent him packing, like the good friend she was, but it did hurt. Then there was the date with James mark two, just last year, which consisted of sitting on his bed watching a game of rugby on TV and was just about as dull as you could get, datewise. Needless to say there wasn't a second.

I looked up at Jake's face, lit in the bright white of a buzzing Roman candle and he sensed me watching him and looked back. He kissed me on the forehead with a proud smile and none of those other boys mattered any more.

Once the fireworks were over, adults mingled and chatted while the younger kids got tired and ratty, bereft of their sparklers. We decided it was time to make our exit, before our parents could be tempted to come over, emboldened by their mulled wine. We were walking towards the rec, when Mark's mum rang to ask him if he'd come home and babysit his little brother.

'I'll come with you,' said Sally and I felt Jake tense slightly.

'Sally, will you just ring Mum quickly and check she doesn't mind, before you rush off?' Jake's tone was a little exasperated and Sally gave him a look. I felt awkward. I'd seen Jake get fatherly like that with Sally before and I knew she hated him being bossy. I'd always sided with Sally before but now things were different. I could see Jake was just being caring, but it still felt a little like I was betraying Sal, standing by Jake's side, holding his hand while he told her off.

After a quick call to get the OK, Sally and Mark headed back towards the house and Mark's car. Jake and I carried on to the rec and sat together on the round-about, a dark playing-field landscape gently turning around us.

'Your mum seems strict about you going into town in the evenings.' I brought the subject up, because I was still thinking about his insistence on Sally making that phone call.

'Actually, she's pretty cool about not making rules,' Jake replied. 'But I know she worries when she doesn't know what we're doing. I think it's worse because Dad's away so much and when she's on her own she worries more, not having the company to take her mind off it.' He paused, but I didn't say anything, I sensed there was more he wanted to say.

'And I worry when she worries. The last thing she needs is to be stressing about us.'

Jake and Sally's mum, Steph, had been diagnosed with breast cancer last year. I remember Sally having a few days off school – she'd been devastated. But they'd found it early, and she'd had a successful operation. She'd been put through a course of chemotherapy and I know Sally found that hard because Steph was ill with it, and of course she lost her hair and everything, so the physical evidence she was ill was right there to be seen. But once the chemo was finished and Steph's hair grew back – she actually looked great with that pixie-short hair. Good cheekbones, Mum said, and Sally soon seemed to be back to her bubbly self.

'I'm actually having a good year,' Jake admitted. 'Working in the shop, making a bit of money. I get a discount on materials, which is great – I can really work on my portfolio . . .' Jake reached for my hand. ' . . . and of course, now, I've had the chance to get to know you better . . . ' He smiled and squeezed my fingers and I smiled back and went pink. 'But the real reason I put off uni was to look out for Mum, so that's what I'm doing. I think Sally forgets sometimes, that's all.'

I realised then that Jake had shouldered all this responsibility. He was stoic and quiet about it, but his dad, Simon, worked so hard and was away so often, he'd sort of become the man of the house. I'd thought of Steph's illness as being over, because that seemed to be how Sally saw it, but of course you have to wait years to get an official all-clear after cancer, and Steph was still having to go for a lot of regular check-ups, which I imagined could be nerve-racking, and it was Jake who drove with her to the hospital.

It was my turn to squeeze Jake's hand, to try to tell him I finally understood why he had to be bossy, to try to tell him that he didn't have to be strong all the time, that I was there for him whenever he needed me. And I think he understood, because he leaned his head on my shoulder and closed his eyes. I stroked his hair and for the first time felt that maybe *I* could make *him* feel safe as well as the other way round.

chapter 5

♥

Jake laughed at me when I opened the door. We were going for a walk and it was cold.

'What?' I asked indignantly, but clearly he was laughing at my woolly hat with its dangly ear-flaps. I loved that hat. It wasn't like I hadn't checked the mirror but I thought it looked kind of funky. Obviously I was horribly, horribly wrong. I'm the first to admit I embrace my inner geek. But sometimes I give her a bit too much in the way of decision-making power. I felt my face flush hot red and reached up to pull off the offending item.

'No!' Jake reached out, grabbed me round the waist and pulled me outside. 'Leave it on. You look cute.' He kissed me right on the hat and then grabbed the braided wool that dangled from the ear-flaps and yanked down on them, laughing again.

'Why are you laughing then?' I whined. 'Jake, I'm not going out if I look like an idiot!'

'No, no you don't, honestly.' Jake was more earnest

now but still a bit smirky and I didn't know whether to trust him or not. I stood sulking, with my hands on my hips. 'Erica, you don't look like an idiot, you look sweet and lovely. Now stop sulking and come on.' He reached behind me and pulled the front door shut, then grinned naughtily and pinned me against it. He held on to the wool braids again with one hand and pushed at my pouting bottom lip with an already freezing thumb. Then he bent down and kissed me insistently. He still made my feet tingle when he kissed me like that – I don't know how he was so strong and so soft at once.

I screwed up my face at him when he released me, and stuck my tongue out. But I couldn't help smiling too and let him pull me by the hand away from the house. It had been raining, but the sun was out brightly and there was that beautiful combination of winter and summer again. We walked quietly, hand in hand, and I couldn't help thinking out loud, 'I love it when it's sunny and there're puddles. It's like there are little bits of sky all over again, shining up at you from the grey of the pavement.'

Jake guffawed loudly, but before I could curse myself for saying what was in my head, he literally swept me off my feet, picking me up and spinning me round. 'You're so weird!' He said it in a way I knew was supposed to be a compliment. 'I love that you can find joy in puddles.'

I loved that I could totally be me with him and he made me feel good about it.

When we got back, I asked if he wanted to come over to mine, but he narrowed his eyes at me. 'You said you had a film essay to write.'

Darn. What did I have to mention that for?

'I do. But it's not due till Wednesday . . . ' I gave him my best puppy dog look.

'I think you should get some of it done at least. I don't want to be the reason you're not doing your work, Erica. Just do a couple of hours on it and give me a call then, OK?' Sometimes I hated how right Jake was all the time. We'd soon worked out a system where I'd take textbooks round and sit at Jake's desk in his room and write my essays on his computer while he drew me. He didn't get a chance to draw life models often like I did at my A-level art classes, and I said I didn't mind him using me for practice – as long as the drawings were flattering! So sometimes he'd mess about and draw me with wings or a halo, or long flowing hair down to my knees, like a Botticelli. But with more clothes on, obviously. He was really talented. I could draw and paint, as in I could get perspective right and make things look reasonably like they did in real life. But Jake had the passion and creativity to go beyond real life and his work had this dream-like, fantasy quality – even his doodles. He'd fill pages of his sketchbook with these strange and beautiful, organic, tangled designs.

When we'd have a tea break, if Sally was around, she would sit on Jake's bedroom floor for half an hour, or we'd hang out in the kitchen and all chat about TV or movies, our college mates or people in the village (everyone knows your business when you live in a village, so you either have to cut yourself off and become a hermit, or just embrace it and join in with the gossip culture). In the evenings Mark would come over and we'd watch movies in Sally's room, or we'd meet up with him in town and go to the cinema, go bowling or just grab a pizza.

But by the end of November, more and more it was just Jake and me. It was really nice to spend time together, just the two of us, but I started to worry that we were leaving Sally out, or even that she was backing off to give us space because she thought that was what we wanted.

One Saturday, I was sitting in my room at my sewing machine, experimenting with the embroidery settings, because I'd decided to sew one of Jake's designs on to a T-shirt for him for his birthday the following weekend and I had a couple of hours before I was supposed to meet Sally and Mark in town. We were going to pick up Jake from swimming and get the train into Cambridge for a gig Jake's mate's band were playing at this Arts Café place. I was just thinking about what I was going to wear and how much I was looking forward to a good night out for the four of us, when my phone beeped.

So sorry guys, M and I can't make 2nite. Explain later. U 2 have fun tho. Sx

I wanted to call her straight back to find out what was going on, and see if I could persuade her to change her mind, but the text seemed odd, like she couldn't talk right then. Jake would probably be in the pool already so I couldn't call him and talk about it either. All I could do was text her back saying I hoped she was OK and to call me when she could. Then I messaged Jake that I'd still meet him at the sports centre and we could walk to the station together, just us two again.

At about seven p.m. Mum dropped me there and offered to take Jake's sports bag home so he didn't have to lug it around all night. He was chuffed at that, and I felt quite pleased too, that Mum would think of it; she obviously trusted Jake to look after me on a night out, but this showed maybe she really liked him too and was happy we were together. Maybe I read too much into it, it wouldn't be the first time – I'm a self-confessed overthinker. I just enjoyed that my parents seemed to treat us like grown-ups.

Anyway, the reason I remember the walk to the station that evening so well, is that when we were halfway there, Jake's friend from the band called to check if we still needed names on the guest list.

'Hello, mate,' Jake replied. 'Ah, sorry, yeah, actually we're two now, not four. My sister's being flaky, but me and my girlfriend are on our way now, so just me plus one would be awesome . . . Thanks, mate . . . Erm, about eight-thirty, what time you on? Cool, yeah see you in a bit. Bye.'

Girlfriend! He used the G-word! Oh, I know it's stupid. It wasn't like I didn't know we were officially going out, but it was the first time he'd said it out loud in front of me and hearing it just felt good. I was grinning into my scarf as Jake stuffed his phone back in his pocket.

'What are you giggling at?' he asked.

'Oh, nothing.'

It was a great night, the band were awesome, Jake's friends were chatty with me and Jake stayed close to me most of the night, as if he was making sure I didn't feel shy on my own. But, looking back, I think that's when things started to change with Sally. She started spending more time in town and I saw less of her. Jake and I talked about it on the train home that night and he shrugged off my worries like he always managed to do. He said Sal was having problems with her grades in politics, and was spending a lot of time studying with this girl from her class, May, and had started staying over sometimes. I'd met May a couple of times and she seemed nice enough, although some of her friends I wasn't so sure about. Still, Jake was usually pretty protective of his sister, so I figured if he wasn't worried, I shouldn't be either.

Then came the distractions of December. Mum still liked to buy me an Advent calendar and for us to decorate the tree together, so I spent much of the evening on Friday 1st doing that (rock and roll, eh?) but it also meant I could finish Jake's T-shirt, because in the morning I wanted to pop into town and get a CD too, so I could go round with all his birthday presents in the afternoon.

The door to Seedies pinged as I pushed it open, and, over the top of the rock section, I spied Mark. I walked round to say hi.

'Mark. What an earth are you doing in *easy listening*?' I said loudly. He swung round and looked only slightly embarrassed.

'Oh, it's my mum's birthday on Monday, she loves rubbish like this. How are you?' He seemed a bit

44

distracted, but I was in a happy, chatty mood so I rambled on.

'I'm good. Hey, that's weird – it's Jake's birthday today as well. I don't know why people have to have birthdays in December, as if it's not hassle enough having to think about everyone's Christmas presents too . . . '

Mark nodded. 'That's right, yeah, I forgot that. You doing anything nice?'

'We're just going for a curry I think, nothing too exciting – you and Sal are welcome to come, I haven't seen you guys for ages.'

Mark turned to face me properly then. He looked confused, and then sort of sad. He glanced down at his feet and sheepishly back up at me through his dark brows.

'Umm. I guess not, or you'd know . . . Sally and I split up. Actually more than a week ago now. I thought you'd have heard, sorry.'

I was stunned and didn't know what to say for a second. He was right, I should have known. But I didn't, and finally it brought home to me how distant Sally and I must have been becoming.

'Oh. Sorry Mark, how embarrassing, I didn't know. I haven't spoken to Sally in a while, college stuff . . . but look, that's no reason you shouldn't come out later if you fancy it – I think a group of us are going. I don't even know if Sally will be there, she's barely been around . . .'

'Thanks, Erica. Actually, I have to go to this family thing tonight anyway – some theatre event, I'm sure it'll be great.' He smiled sarcastically and then backed towards the till, gesturing with the CD in his hand. 'I'd better get this and make a move. Thanks though. Have fun tonight.'

I could have cried. What was going on? Just a couple of months before, it would have been unthinkable that something this huge could happen in Sally's life without her telling me. I thought about that text she'd sent me and wondered how long she been planning to avoid coming to the gig. I didn't know what to think. Should I be kicking myself for doing something wrong and losing her, or for being too wrapped up in Jake to even know what was happening? Or should I be upset or angry with her because she'd probably confided in May instead of me, and because she'd practically been lying to us?

Seeing Jake's face when he opened his presents cheered me up.

'Erica, it's amazing. Perfect, thank you,' he said when he saw his design on the T-shirt. He hugged me tightly and kissed me all over my face, which made me laugh. But before long I had to bring up that I'd seen Mark, and Jake was stumped too, and couldn't understand why we hadn't heard. But he just told me again that Sally had seemed preoccupied with work and maybe she'd decided to put her social life on hold while she sorted her grades out.

I knew Sally was ambitious about being a lawyer, but I thought about splitting with Jake, the best thing in my life, for the sake of grades, and it didn't make any sense to me. I wondered if he knew more than I did and I was reading too much into it, or if he was in denial of parental proportions. But there wasn't any point spoiling the evening arguing about it. I'd just have to speak to Sally.

So the next night, when Mum and Dad were watching a movie after dinner, I slipped into the dining room and turned on the computer. Just a couple of weeks before, I wouldn't have thought of emailing Sally. If I'd wanted to speak to her I'd have just picked up the phone. But everything was odd. I was worried about her, but I felt frozen out and couldn't tell her what I was feeling over the phone. Somehow it would have been hard, and, weirdest of all, I think I'd have felt I was invading her privacy. So I clicked 'Compose Mail' and wrote:

My Best Friend's Brother

Hey stranger. Hope you're OK, feel like I
haven't seen you in for ever. What you doing
next Saturday? Christmas is looming and I think
some shopping is in order - fancy a trip to
London? We could make a day of it, grab some
lunch and have a proper catch up. Dad said he'd
drop us at the station and even shout us the
train tickets - guess it's got to the stage
where he'll actually pay money to get rid of
me!! Take advantage, I say. Please say yes.

xxxE

Chapter 6

♥

In the morning there was a reply waiting in my inbox.

```
Hello lovely. Shopping day sounds fab, I'm in.
Skint though, so I've got a budget and you have
to promise to wrestle me to the ground the
minute I start making for the cashpoint, OK?
Sx
```

I was elated that her reply was chatty and normal – and that she'd said yes. But I wasn't sure what I was going to do about broaching the subject of her and Mark. Part of me thought I should wait for the right moment, and not spoil the day, but I also knew I'd be on edge wanting to ask her.

When Saturday came and we were on the platform at the train station, arms linked, braced against the cold, everything felt familiar again and it seemed right to bring it up. I just tried to keep it chatty.

'I bumped into Mark last weekend in Seedies making out he was buying his mum this cheesy coffee table jazz CD, although I'm sure he was eyeing it up for himself.'

I waited for a reaction, but Sally buried her nose

further into her scarf and scuffed her heels sheepishly on the wet ground. The Sally I knew would give in with a little push, so I tried again. 'How come you didn't tell me?' I asked, as gently as I could.

'Oh, there was nothing to tell really.' She sounded sad but philosophical. 'We were seeing each other out of habit as much as really wanting to. We grew apart, you know, all that old stuff. We weren't like you and Jake. I'm OK, honestly, otherwise I would have told you.'

I wasn't sure.

'I don't get it, you seemed happy still, when you were together.' I felt a bit odd the way she'd mentioned me and Jake – the words sounded like they should have been a compliment, but her tone was strained, almost as if she was blaming us or being aggressive. 'But if you're sure you're OK . . . ?'

'Really.' Sally turned to look me in the eye. 'Of course I feel a bit sad, but that's all. It's for the best, I'll be fine, really.'

And that was that. I was relieved. It didn't seem so strange after all that she hadn't mentioned it. I figured it wasn't the sort of thing you'd just text or call to say out of the blue unless you needed to talk, and she seemed to be dealing with it. I did feel a certain loss that she could cope without me though, we'd always gone through these things together. I wondered if it was just that we were getting older.

On the train, we got busy talking shopping and budgets, looking at our *A to Z* and planning the day. Sally suggested heading to St Christopher's Place for lunch and popping into her dad's office to see if he was around. He worked most Saturdays.

'It's really near Selfridges, which we'd want to go to anyway, then maybe he'll buy us lunch and we can save some cash,' she grinned at me. I agreed, thinking for a moment that it would have been nice not to have to be on best lunch-with-the-parents behaviour but hey, why say no to a free meal?

The morning was fun, if a bit exhausting with all the crowds to struggle through, but we were doing well and were slowly becoming laden with all our purchases. By one p.m. we were ready for a rest and some nourishment. We headed to Sally's dad's office but, when the receptionist rang up to his desk, a colleague told her he'd gone out already. We spotted a café just across the street as we headed back out through the revolving doors, and Sally suggested we got some drinks and sat by the window, so we could keep an eye out in case he came back in the next fifteen minutes. I knew she was skint but it did seem a bit odd that she was so intent on seeing him, when presumably he'd be back at home that night anyway.

She must have sensed my hesitation because then she said, 'It just seems a shame to come up here and not say hi – we'd be sitting in a café anyway, so what's the difference?' She'd obviously made up her mind and it didn't really matter to me, so I went along with it.

Well, we did see him come back to the office. Sally was telling me about why Jade Jackson hadn't been at May's party the previous weekend. Nadine had basically decided Jade was after her boyfriend, Max, because she'd been seen speaking to him (gasp) at the football in the morning and, drama queen that she was, she'd blown it up into this huge thing and, because May was Nadine's new best friend, she'd sided with her and started freezing Jade out. Sally was just describing how she found Jade crying in the toilets after law when I saw Sally's dad. Without giving myself time to think, I interrupted Sally and pointed over.

I've wondered so many times since, how things could have been different if I'd kept quiet and waited just a minute, just long enough to see what was happening before I made Sally look . . . by the time she turned round, you could see the woman he was talking to wasn't an ordinary colleague or client. They were holding hands. She was gazing up at him, smiling. As they stopped in a darkened doorway not five metres from the office, they pulled back into the shadow, although not so far that you couldn't see his arm encircle her waist as she tilted her head up towards him and they kissed.

Sally was perfectly still, fingertips still clasping the yellow and white straw she'd been stabbing at the ice in her Diet Coke with, but staring. It may have been the grey winter light seeping through the window, but her face seemed ashen.

For a moment I was just as paralysed. I couldn't do anything but watch as Sally glared, as the couple said goodbye and walked their separate ways, her dad glancing around as he slipped back through those glass doors and disappeared into a lift. Sally didn't speak, so I did. Idiotic nonsense spilled out of my mouth as I tried to second-guess what she was thinking.

'Maybe she's a client. He has to help people who have been through really horrible things a lot, doesn't he? Maybe he was comforting her – or if she's a close colleague and they're good friends but she's having a hard time or something – maybe she's getting fired or something and they're saying goodbye . . . ' But that hadn't been a goodbye kiss or a comforting kiss, and she hadn't looked in the least bit upset. Neither of them had.

'Don't jump to conclusions, Sal. How about we go in, say hello, mention that we saw her – he can explain who she was . . . '

I could see the tears in Sally's eyes and I could see she was swallowing hard against her emotions. Without warning she jumped up, her chair legs screeching against the floor tiles, grabbed her bag and ran out of the café. She wasn't stopping. In a panic, I scrabbled to get all my stuff, and the shopping bag Sally had left under the table, remembered we hadn't paid for our drinks, searched desperately through my pockets for a tatty fiver which I waved at the woman behind the counter and threw on to the table before I clumsily pulled the door open and ran after her, coat and scarf trailing on the ground, not a spare hand to put them on despite the cold. I saw Sally disappear down a narrow side street on the other side of the square, leading back into the throng of stressed shoppers, and cursed under my breath as I lolloped after her as fast as I could.

Back on Oxford Street though, I lost her in the crowd. Scanning up and down the street, trying to work out which way she'd gone, I tried to cross the pavement for a better view, pushing through tutting, shoving currents of people. Just as tears of frustration were pricking my eyes, a bus slowed as it passed me and pulled in at the next stop. Thank goodness I followed it with my eyes, because then I saw Sally in the queue of people squashing to get on. I ran, and reached her just as she was getting to the doors.

'Sally! Wait, please . . . ' was all I could say as I tried breathlessly to reach out to her, shopping bags swinging wildly. I was crying. Guilty-faced, she moved away from the bus towards me and gave in to tears too. Seeing a stone bench a few steps away, I took the chance to grab a space to rest, released the bags, beckoned to Sally, and we hugged.

We sat, waiting for the next bus, both knowing it was time to go home. And Sally apologised.

'I'm sorry, Erica. I shouldn't have run off like that'.

'It's OK,' I reassured her. 'It was a shock to see that, I guess, but there could be an explanation you know.'

Sally shook her head. 'To be honest, it wasn't that much of a shock.' She waited for the confusion to register on my face. 'I've sort of known for a while Dad was up to something. It's part of the reason I wanted to surprise him. I'd imagined seeing exactly what we saw, and that I'd confront him with the proof once I had it. But when it really happened it hit me harder than I thought and I was just too weak and pathetic and scared to go and shout at him like I'd thought I would.'

I remembered all Jake had told me about what his mum had been through with her illness and I was angry with Sally's dad for doing this after everything else the family had had to cope with. He deserved to be shouted at.

'We could still go back you know, or we could wait, and go and meet him when he's done for the day. You could still tell him everything you need to tell him – you must be so angry, Sal, I'm sorry.'

'You know, I'm really not as angry as I thought I'd be. More sad, and scared. I wouldn't know what to do if he left, Erica. It can't happen – I have to fix it.'

I was confused by what was going on in her head, but then I saw the bus coming and we had to make a decision. 'Do you want to stay? Or go home?' I asked Sally. She looked so dejected and I was helpless to make her feel better.

'Let's go. I think that's enough drama for one day, don't you?' She smiled weakly and we bundled on the bus just as half-hearted rain started spitting at the windows. We climbed up to the top deck and for a while we just watched, silently, as the streets swarmed with the stressed, frowning people amongst all the over-cheery Christmas glitz below us.

On the train, I admit I pushed Sally to talk a bit more. She seemed lost inside herself, but I needed to know what she was thinking. I used to be able to guess pretty well, but that had changed.

'Are you going to tell your mum?' I asked.

'God, no!' Sally seemed almost angry, and I shrank back a little. She reached for my hand and spoke in an urgent whisper: 'Listen, Erica, this is a secret, OK? I know I can trust you, but you have to know how important this is – no one needs to know about what we saw until I've found out exactly what's happening. And, listen, you can't talk to Jake about this, OK?'.

I couldn't understand what she was planning – maybe it was just too hard for her to admit what she'd seen and now she was backtracking.

'But Sal, he's the one person you could really talk to about it, who'd understand, and knows your parents – you could decide what to do together – otherwise you're going through it all alone ... '

She let go of my hand and held her face in frustration. 'We wouldn't decide together, though, would we? You know what Jake's like – he always has an idea about what's right and he thinks he knows better than anyone. Besides, I know exactly what he'd want to do: he'd go straight to Mum. Sometimes I think he hates Dad, that he wants him gone – but that's fine for him, he's Mum's favourite anyway and he doesn't care what I'd feel like ... '

'Of course he cares!' She was being so unfair to Jake. 'He'll listen if you just explain to him what you're feeling.'

Sally gasped back a sob then, and I felt confused and clueless. 'Erica, listen to me, OK? I mean this. Jake's different with you . . . oh, never mind. I know you're looking out for me, but this is not your stuff – I mean, it's my family and I know you want to help but you can't understand it, not really. What happened today is my secret, OK, it's not yours to tell Jake – you CANNOT tell him, OK?'

I nodded and mumbled an 'of course' or two. I told her I'd do whatever she wanted, but I was shocked by the way she was about it all. I worried how I'd be with Jake that evening without talking about it. But I couldn't even begin, back then, to imagine how hard it was going to be.

Chapter 7

♥

When Jake came to the door that night, I hugged him hard, burrowing my face in his shoulder.

'You all right?' He looked a bit bemused and stroked away the hair from my face when I finally let him go.

'Yeah.' I smiled and we headed up to my room. 'I'm just glad to see you.'

'How was shopping?' Jake dropped himself on to my bed and I returned to my carefully arranged present-wrapping station on the floor.

'Oh, fine,' I said with a little sigh that maybe wasn't too discreet now I think about it.

'Are you sure?' he persisted. 'Did you and Sal have an argument? She was being moody in her room when I got in and you seem a bit weird too.'

Oops.

'No, no, I'm fine – it was good.' I desperately hoped I wasn't blushing. (Can you take lying classes? If not, they should start doing them. I could really do with better skills in that department.) 'It was just kind of exhausting, you know how the shops can be in London on a Saturday. Anyway, it's a girl's privilege to be moody in her room sometimes.' I smiled my best cheeky smile at him to distract him from the subject. 'She probably had wrapping to do too, with all the stuff we got today. Now, be good while I finish these.' I got away with it I think.

I'd hidden Jake's presents away and had a few family ones to wrap before I could tick them all off my list. I loved the excitement of wrapping everyone's presents, making them look nice and imagining them in their little piles under the tree. I'd just wrapped a liquid eyeliner pen for Tamara and was tying ribbon round it as Jake watched. I reached for the scissors and pulled the flat of the ribbon along the blade so it curled up into a little flounce.

'Are you going to do that with every single teeny tiny little present?' Jake was smirking at me again and I plonked the scissors down in a mock huff.

'Half the fun of Christmas is planning your present-wrapping colour scheme and accessories!' Smirk. 'It's just as important to give as receive, Jake Earley.' I picked the scissors back up and brandished them at him. 'And frankly, if you're not wrapping with love, you're missing out.' I proudly curled the other end of the ribbon and started on the next gift.

He leaned over and ruffled my hair in a deliberately patronising way and then switched on the TV and waited obediently while I finished, but by the time I'd wrapped my last one, a Brahms CD for Dad, he was fast asleep.

I packed up my bows and tags as quietly as I could and moved over to sit by the bed where I could see the TV. But if I'm honest I was more interested in watching Jake's perfect, sleeping face. I think I could have happily just watched him be still for a full half-hour. If I had somehow been able to go back in time to visit my September self, and describe this scene to her, she would never have believed it. Jake was mine, and there he was, dozing comfortably *in my bedroom, on my bed!*

The next day, Tamara arrived home for the holiday and, for all the worrying I'd done about being back in baby-of-the-family mode, it was actually nice to be the little sister again. It was good to sit around the dinner table, all four of us together. Obviously I'd told her about Jake and me and it was embarrassing when he came over and she tousled his hair and winked at him like he was a cheeky toddler. But I knew she approved, and that it was affectionate, so I let her off.

Term finished on December 20th and Jake called that night when he got in from work.

'Wanna come over?' I asked.

'Why don't you come to me for a change?' Jake said. 'I'm knackered. And I'm sure your mum and dad are getting sick of me turning up on your doorstep.'

He had a point. I'd been finding excuses not to go over there. Things had been weird between Sally and me. When we had coffee in the canteen at break, or saw each other at lunch, we'd make small talk, almost like strangers. We were avoiding the real subject. She seemed happier when she was with May and Nadine. So, more and more, I'd sit with Ruth and Charlotte and leave them to it. I was nervous of what it would be like if we saw each other in her house. I couldn't predict how it would be. But I knew it would probably be obvious to Jake something was different. I clearly wasn't getting away with avoiding it any longer, though. I had to risk it, because if I started refusing to go over there without saying why, that would definitely give the game away anyway. I bit my lip.

'OK, sure. I'll come to you. See you in a bit.'

It was noisy when I got there and I had to knock a few times. Steph answered the door eventually, with a dripping whisk in her hand and flour in her eyebrow.

'Hi, Erica. Sorry love, the kiddies are having a bit of a music war up there, I think! Go on up.'

I smiled thanks as she rushed back to her cooking and I braved the stairs. I could just about hear Sally humming along to The Killers as I crept past her room. Then, as I moved closer to Jake's slightly open door, there was a horrible moment of a morphing clash of guitars and drums and then I was listening to Muse.

'Oh! Hey gorgeous. You snuck in quietly.' Jake looked up from his sketchpad as I peered through the door. He beckoned for me to come in. 'I left my door open so I'd hear you knock, but . . . ' He jumped up, charcoal-blackened hands held up in the air, and kissed me quickly before heading out on to the landing. 'I'll just wash these.' I saw Sally dart out of her bedroom and into the bathroom at lightning speed before Jake could get there, and I retreated further back into the room. 'Nice! I'll use the kitchen sink then, shall I?' I heard Jake shout though the door.

A minute and a half later I heard Sally click off the bathroom light and pass Jake on the stairs.

'Erica's here,' Jake said.

'Kind of in a hurry, bro, you'll have to say hi for me.'

When I heard the door slam I didn't know whether to

feel relieved she'd gone, or hurt that she couldn't spare a minute to say hi. Still, I suppose I could have knocked on my way in instead of running straight to Jake's room, if I wasn't such a scaredy-cat.

'Sally says hi,' said Jake as he came back into the room. I nodded but didn't say anything. I felt this wave of sadness hit me and had to grit my teeth against crying. Of course Jake noticed.

'There's something going on with you two, isn't there? What is it?' He sat down close to me and put his arm round my waist. (Why did he have to be so perceptive? I thought men were supposed to be dunces about emotional girl-stuff.) I held on to him tightly and fought back tears. I wanted to tell him everything, so badly. We told each other our secrets. The reason I was so happy when we were together was that we could be totally open and relaxed. I'd never held anything back before and it felt wrong. It felt painful, like I was betraying myself as well as him. I opened my mouth to speak – after this latest snub from Sally I was so close to spilling the whole story. But I didn't.

'Oh, I'm just being silly.' I sniffed. 'Sorry.' I sat up straighter. Seeing Jake's concerned face, I couldn't help putting a hand up to his cheek and giving him a kiss. 'Sally's just spending a lot of time with May and Nadine these days and I'm not really friendly with them so it means we're apart a lot. It's just taking a bit of getting used to, that's all. It's fine.'

Jake seemed satisfied with my answer and pouted in sympathy with me. 'Well, I'm not really friendly with May and Nadine either, so you've always got me.' He gave me a cheesy-grin-and-eyebrow-wiggle double-whammy and got another kiss in return.

Relatives descended on both the Mitford and Earley households on Christmas Eve, and 'family time' meant I wouldn't see Jake for a couple of days – thank the Lord for mobile phones.

On Christmas morning I woke to feel a heavy rustling as I moved my feet. In half sleep, I felt like a little kid again, waking to find a stocking full of presents on top of the covers at the end of the bed, weighing down deliciously on my toes. As I came round properly I looked down – and it was real. There really was a stocking there. Not the hand-knitted Christmas stocking of my childhood though, a red felt one with a proper white-fluff-trimmed top. There was no mistaking it.

Had Mum gone crazy? We hadn't had these since I was twelve. I wondered if she had that middle-aged offspring-flying-the-nest angst thing my dad joked about when Tamara went off to uni. But I knew Mum wasn't that type. Then for a minute I even suspected Tamara too, thinking maybe she'd gone soft, but that didn't seem likely either. So I figured, since my limbs had woken up by this point, there was only one way to get to the bottom of this. Allowing myself some childlike Christmas glee, I reached down, grabbed the stocking and delved in.

The first present was a flat little box about the size of my palm, wrapped in silver and with curly gold ribbon around it. I looked at the tag. It was from Jake! How had he got this stocking on my bed? He'd either colluded with Mum, or Dad was going to have something to say about him sneaking into my room in the night.

For Erica,
This one's from the day we walked through the
churchyard and you spotted this and said you liked
it because it reminded you of my drawings.
Christmas kisses, Jake.

Later, in a different pen, he'd added at the bottom: *(wrapped with love).*

I laughed out loud. Then I practically cried at the romance of it, looking at all the other little presents, each with their careful curly ribbons and tags. I opened the one I was holding and found the brooch that had been sitting in a shop window as we'd walked past it that day I remembered well. I still loved it. It was plain silver but with an intricate, twirly design.

It was like Jake had bought all these little presents whenever he'd seen anything he thought I'd like and saved them all up just for this occasion. They all had notes attached: the lip balm he knew was my favourite, *To keep you in good kissing order*; some sparkly threads and beads *To make your clever girl-things with*; and my favourite fancy chocolate *'Cos I know you can't last the day without your sugar fix*. And all of them, *(wrapped with love)*.

I hadn't thought it possible that I could love Jake more, but I was aching with the strength of it then. I wanted to run up the street and find him and hold him. I grabbed my phone and turned it on, impatiently waiting for it to be ready. I opened a new message and wrote: *I love my presents. I love you. Thank you. Merry Christmas. Xxxxxxx*.

My finger hovered over the 'Send' button for a moment. It was quite scary – we hadn't said it before, the 'love' thing, but it was what I was feeling and I wanted him to know it. So I pressed.

A tense nine minutes later, there was a bleep.

I love mine too. And I love you too. And Merry Christmas too. Xxxx.

I was soooo happy I can't describe it. I hugged my duvet round me and just stared at that message, practically stroking the phone, for who knows how long, until Tamara barged in with barely so much as two seconds' warning. Mum had told her about helping sneak the stocking into my room and so of course she came straight up to be nosy.

In the afternoon I even got a text from Sally, just saying Happy Christmas. She probably sent it out to her whole phonebook, but I took it as a sign she didn't hate me at least. I texted back and said I hoped to see her soon.

Boxing Day passed in a food-filled blur and, the day after that, Mum and Dad went back to work and Christmas started to feel over, but I had buckets of chocolates and a brand new DVD from my cousin, so I texted Sally and Jake to see if they wanted to come over. Tam seemed up for watching it so I figured it'd be like old times if Sally and Jake came over and we could all have a catch-up and hang out. When Jake replied: *Be over in 15 xx* and I didn't hear back from Sally, I assumed he meant both of them, I don't know why. But when I opened the door to him, he was alone. Sally had gone to May's. And in the end Tam went out to the sales, so it ended up just Jake and me. It was lovely, curled up on the sofa together with the house to ourselves, but it just wasn't the reunion I'd imagined.

Chapter 8

♥

I was really excited about New Year's Eve. Jake's mate Rich was having a party in the village, with loads of people staying, so it turned out a lot of our friends from town were coming over to us for a change and we wouldn't have to worry about lifts – we could just wander up the road, see friends and have a drink, and not have to worry about how much money the cab home would cost. And Sally was coming. She'd actually left me a really sweet voicemail saying she hoped I was going and that it would be lovely to see me properly finally. We'd arranged that I'd go over to her place and we'd get ready together.

I turned up ridiculously early at about six p.m. feeling quite nervous. But Sally answered the door with a big hug, got us drinks and snacks and then rushed me upstairs to help her choose what to wear. When Jake knocked she said it was girls only, just for an hour, and he should 'go play with his toys' until we were beautified. We talked about who was coming to the party, and whether Rich's ex and his new girlfriend would be there, and whether I should wear my hair up or down – it felt so like old times that, for a while, I forgot all that had happened in the past few weeks.

I was so happy walking up the road to Rich's, my right arm linked through Jake's and my left through Sally's. We were all shivering, and although it was freezing I knew, for me, it was partly the anticipation of the night ahead that was making me trembly. After a classic family Christmas indoors it'd be great to catch up with everyone – and dance. Sally must have read my mind, because it suddenly occurred to her to ask about the music.

'Hey Jake, is Rich doing his DJ thing tonight?' she tried to sound nonchalant but there was an obvious tinge of concern in her voice, although I didn't think Jake had cottoned on.

'No, there's quite a lot of people coming and I think he was worried about his decks getting damaged so I think he's just going to plug people's MP3 players straight into the stereo.'

'Oh, that's good,' Sally and I said at exactly the same time, with such blatant relief in our voices that we couldn't help laughing. Jake looked at us though mock-cross eyebrows.

'You women are so evil! He only got his decks in

September. I think he's pretty good, considering.'

'Considering his horrible, horrible taste in music, you mean?' Sally grinned, and I nudged her with another giggle.

We were quite early and there must have been less than ten people when we got there, I think. I managed to calm Sally's impatience by pointing out we had our run of the buffet, which was actually quite impressive, and there was a pretty steady stream of people arriving, so the place was bustling before we knew it.

Rich and his brother James had cleared a lot of furniture out of their massive living room and, once someone had swapped their iPod in for Rich's, loads of people were dancing. Jake and I danced a couple of times, but I was mostly dancing with the girls and catching up with school friends in the kitchen. We had such a good time I'd barely noticed how late it was, but at five to midnight the music went off and we put the TV on, ready to watch Big Ben.

When the chimes were about to start, I scanned the room for Jake but within seconds I felt his arm slip round my waist as he came through from the kitchen behind me. I smiled over my shoulder at him and leaned into him, feeling complete and happy and hopeful. At the twelfth chime, everyone cheered. Party poppers went off and people jumped up and down, hugging each other and shouting 'Happy New Year!'

Jake and I kissed and he looked into my eyes and whispered, 'Happy New Year, gorgeous.' As I grinned at him, Sally came over and hugged us in a group embrace and kissed us both. Then Ruth practically ran into me out of nowhere and enveloped me in a bear hug. While Jake did a lot of manly shoulder slapping with the boys, the music came back on and the shouts died back down into general party noise. That's when I spotted Sally, bundling out of the door with Ed, Munch, Nadine, May and some of their friends I didn't recognise, who looked quite a bit older.

I stepped into Rich's path as he came over towards the kitchen.

'Where are that lot going?' I tried not to sound cross.

'Who?' he shouted over the music.

'Nadine and Munch and that lot.' I nodded towards the door.

'Oh, they're going on to some club in town, I think.' I followed as he pushed through to the kitchen. 'Davy said he reckoned some mate of his who works there'll be able to sneak them in for free now it's gone midnight. Don't reckon it'll be much good though now, just the drunken dregs left, if you know what I mean. You're better off staying here and helping me get through the rest of these sausage rolls – reckon there's only about twenty million left now!' His voice tailed off as his head disappeared into the fridge for another drink.

He sounded like he thought I was jealous and wanted to go to the club. All I actually wanted was for Sally to come back. I didn't trust that lot. Ed and Munch always seemed like they were chasing trouble and, although May was nice when she was on her own, Nadine was a drama junkie. Like all that business with Jade, she never seemed bothered about other people's feelings; she seemed to stir things up deliberately just to create excitement for herself. I felt riled up and had to reason with myself. Maybe I was being unfair, I didn't really know them. But I just couldn't help feeling uncomfortable thinking Sally was out with them. Then it occurred to me, all the time Sally had spent with May lately, this was probably a regular thing – and Sally had seemed fine tonight so it obviously wasn't doing her any harm. What right did I have to get Mumsy about it now, just because I'd happened to see them leaving? Argh. That was the worst thing about it – I felt like such a saddo geek judging them and worrying. Maybe it was *me* I needed to worry about, feeling about ready to go home when it was barely half past twelve.

I found Jake by the stairs, having the end of a

conversation with Ruth as she headed to the bathroom. As I walked up to him, he reached out with a strong arm and pulled me in towards him, kissing my forehead.

'Hey,' I said quietly, feeling really tired suddenly. 'Did you know Sal went into town with May and that lot?'

'Yeah.' He rolled his eyes. 'I had to give her the last of my cash so she can get home. Can't see the attraction myself, but I guess she wants to have some fun before you kids have to go back to school.' He winked at me, trying to get away with calling me 'kid' in the name of comedy, but he still got a girl-punch in the stomach for that.

By the time we left, the house was emptying. As a wave of bodies and noise receded, a mess of cans and cups, ashtrays and dirty paper plates was revealed, like debris washed up on a beach. Outside, though, the air was crisp and cold and clean. The not-quite-full moon was beautifully bright and Jake and I huddled together as we slowly walked home. It must have been about one a.m. The few lights that were still on were shut away cosily inside their warm houses and our little cul-de-sac was silent as usual, despite the occasion. In the perfect quiet I felt like the world was ours, just for a few minutes.

Then I noticed Jake's forehead was furrowed a little.

'You OK?' I asked, squeezing his hand.

'Ruth was asking if there was something going on

between Sally and Ed. I said no, but Sally wouldn't tell me that stuff anyway. Do you know?'

I was genuinely surprised, but I had to admit I didn't know either. 'I don't *think* so. But, you know, when we were having such a good time getting ready tonight, it felt for a while like it used to, when Sal and I were so close – but I guess it was sort of an illusion. Before tonight, I can't remember the last time we really sat and talked, so I don't think she'd tell me either – she didn't even tell me when she and Mark broke up, remember? I just don't see that much of her at the moment.'

'That's what Ruth said too,' frowned Jake. 'I just figured she'd been hanging out with May – but I didn't know she was mates with Ed. Rich hates him – I think they've got some history or something. I never really paid much attention before, but I'm not sure how I feel about Sal being with him. And Ruth seemed worried too, like Sal was going off the rails or something. Am I being blind, Erica, is there something going on with her?'

I felt sick. My heart was thumping. Of course there was something going on with her. She was terrified her family was falling apart and she was trying to deal with it. The thought of it made me sob and I couldn't stop myself.

'Oh, oh, I'm sorry, I didn't mean to upset you.' Jake swept me into a strong hug. I had to tell him.

'She won't talk to me about it, Jake. I don't know what to do . . . ' I cried. But he misunderstood.

'I know. I'm sorry. I don't know why I'm quizzing you like that when you don't know any more than me. Don't worry. I'll talk to Rich about Ed. I'm sure it's fine. He's probably just better at football – Rich is such a kid about that stuff.' He held my face and smoothed my hair out of my wet eyes, and kissed me. 'Don't worry,' he repeated. I was shaking. 'You're freezing, come on, I'll walk you to your door.'

I stayed quiet and just said 'Happy New Year' again when Jake did, and 'good-night' when Jake did; and I went to bed queasy with confusion. I'd come so close to betraying Sally's trust. So close, I was ashamed of myself. But now that Jake was starting to worry about her too, it was harder to pretend everything was fine. And it was so hard to lie to Jake. And even though I *wasn't* really lying to him, it felt like I was, and it felt horrible.

Term started on Wednesday 3rd, and on the Friday Ruth threw a dinner party at hers as a kind of commiseration on being put to work again. I'd said I'd drive Sally because Jake was going into town too for a night out with some mates, and was taking their car and staying overnight. When I knocked on their door, Steph answered. She looked tired. She said Sally would be ready in a minute so we sat in the kitchen together while Sal clattered about upstairs. Steph was drinking some sort of evil-looking green sludge, wheatgrass and ginger something-or-other I think, so when she offered me a drink I instinctively declined, although I'm sure she would have poured me a water or made tea.

'What are you up to tonight then?' she asked.

I told her just dinner at Ruth's, not a late one, and just as a puzzled look flickered across her face, Sally skipped down the stairs, grabbed her bag and went straight for the door.

'Sorry Erica, I've made us a bit late – you ready? We should probably get going. Hey Mum, see you later, don't wait up!'

I hesitated for a second, then shrugged at Steph and followed Sally, who was already at the car with her hand poised on the handle. She had on chunky high heels and a teeny tunic dress. Her hair was big and backcombed and she had loads of black eye make-up on. She looked amazing, but a bit overdressed for dinner at Ruth's, and I had a sinking feeling as our seatbelt fasteners clicked into place and we drove off.

'You look nice,' I said, hoping she'd offer an explanation.

'Oh, thanks hon,' was all she said.

'Ruth'll be flattered you've made such an effort,' I said, humourlessly I admit, because I knew what was coming.

'Oh, I'm meeting up with May and Nadine after dinner. I'm not sure where we're going, so I thought I'd better not wear jeans and trainers just in case . . . ' She looked down at my black skinny jeans and Vans. 'Er, but if we don't end up going anywhere special, you know, with a dress code, you're welcome to come . . . '

I knew she didn't mean it.

'I think I'd feel a bit underdressed anyway, though – maybe next time,' I said. I thought about what she'd said to Steph as we'd left her house. 'Does your mum think you're coming home with me?' I asked her.

She was the worst liar. 'Erm, no, I don't think so. I did say I'd be out late. I'll make sure I tell her if I have to get a taxi back, don't worry.'

Dinner was embarrassing. We tried to ignore Sally's obvious impatience to leave – she was practically still chewing as she walked out of the door – but I felt bad for Ruth after all the effort she'd made. Her parents had even made themselves scarce for the evening so we could have a proper gossip. And to be honest, I felt bad for me too. I didn't like feeling angry with Sal, I didn't like that she wasn't interested in spending time with us any more, and

I didn't like that the Sally I *did* like seemed to be slipping away.

It was a nice evening once she'd gone; we watched some TV but mostly chatted about our uni applications and our plans for next year. Ruth and Charlotte were excited about how little college we had left, how soon they'd be moving out of home and starting new lives. Of course, I was too, but a part of me hadn't quite acknowledged yet that it was all going to be so soon. I was morbidly nervous about what would happen. My first choice was Brighton, and, although Jake had his place at Edinburgh to take up, I knew he wasn't sure if he wanted to go back into studying. He was actually pretty happy working at the shop because it meant he was well connected to get his work sold and exhibited locally. He was already making money from his paintings, so there didn't seem to be much reason for him to keep training as long as he was doing as well as he was. As I drove home alone, I felt isolated and nervous about the changes that seemed to be going on around me. It all seemed beyond my control.

Chapter 9

♥

I shut my eyes against the tingle of tears. I couldn't be crying just because Jake was going away for a week! I couldn't have turned *that* soppy. I wasn't jealous at all that he'd be skiing in France while I was stuck at home – I'd been skiing once and it had been embarrassing enough to last me a lifetime. But we'd been together over three months and this was the first time he wouldn't be just round the corner if I wanted to see him. And with things going wrong with Sally, and the winter blues and all, I guess it all got a bit much. That's my excuse anyway. Thankfully, Jake was being pretty soppy too.

'I kind of wish I wasn't going now,' he said, squeezing me tightly.

'You do not,' I said, finding it easier to be tough while he was being so cute. 'You'll have a great time. Besides, I've driven you to the flipping airport now, so if you don't get on the plane I'm going to charge you petrol money.'

His mates had flown out early that morning, but Jake

was a late addition to the group because he'd had to work during the day, so he was stuck for a ride to catch his later flight and I said I'd drive him. I waited while he checked in, just to draw the whole thing out, and we hugged goodbye again at the bottom of the escalator up to departures. We kissed and Jake held my face in his hands.

'I'll miss you,' he said. God, I almost cried again.

'I'll miss you too,' I said. And, having to joke to keep my senses, said 'Now sod off!' I pretended to push him on to the escalator and he pretended that I could actually push him on to the escalator if I wanted. He stuck his bottom lip out and waved at me as he disappeared backwards and upwards. I laughed and waved back, then slowly turned and headed towards the car park. Thank God I was going to Anna Harrison's party that night, or I'd be properly moping. As it was, I had to rush back, shower and make some serious wardrobe decisions.

Mum said she'd drop us off and pick us up to save us driving or worrying about cabs, so I texted Sally at seven-thirty and told her to be outside for eight. She was leaning against the car when we came out of the house, dressed all in black and looking great, but tired, and as if she'd lost weight.

The party was at the function hall at the Broadwick Hotel, where the Hallowe'en ball had been, and, as we drove up, there was 'our' bench. It pulled at my heart to see it but made me smile too. I obviously wasn't going to be able to forget about Jake tonight.

It was packed and noisy inside. The music was great and we had loads of fun to start with. I didn't see much of Sally, but Ruth and Charlotte and I were dancing loads. By eleven-thirty I felt tired. It was half an hour till Mum was due to come and get us, but I was keen to get outside in plenty of time so I went in search of Sally to see if she was about ready. I couldn't find her. As I came out of the Ladies and walked through the lobby, I felt like some air, so went outside to sit on the bench for a bit. I was thinking about Jake anyway so I figured I might as well indulge myself.

Well, there was Sally. She was leaning against a wall beside the car park, smoking, and Ed was with her, his hand on her bum, kissing her neck. She didn't look all that interested but she wasn't exactly fighting him off either . . . and I was sure he had a new girlfriend. I was rooted to the spot. This was a different girl to the Sally I knew. What was going on?

Munch and Nadine appeared round the corner and the four of them seemed to huddle for a moment before making off towards the town centre. Nice of Sally to let me know she didn't need a lift after all. I felt like giving up on her right then, on just deciding if I wasn't important to her any more then she wasn't worth my time. But the feeling didn't last long before I started to blame myself. She was keeping this huge secret, terrified her family would be torn apart. I was the only person who could help her because I was the only other person who knew. She was going through all this pain and I was about to abandon her. No matter how strangely she was acting, she was still Sally, my best friend for what felt like our whole lives.

When Mum pulled up I had to explain Sally had gone. We drove back and forth through the town centre for a while, but there was no sign of them and Sally's mobile was going straight through to answerphone, which made me think she'd either run out of battery or they'd gone to The Studio, a notoriously rough basement club where she wouldn't have any signal. Mum called Steph and while they were chatting Steph got a text from Sally, from a number she didn't recognise, saying they were at a party and she'd be staying at May's. I didn't know how much of the truth she was hiding but at least we could go home.

'What is going on with that girl, Erica? Mum asked.

'I don't know, mum, I really don't.' All my emotion came pouring out. 'I don't know what I can do – I hardly really see her any more anyway. I mean we go out together, but she's not really there, and then after a while she goes off with May's crowd . . . '

Mum could tell I was worried and her voice softened. 'Don't worry, love, it's not up to you to sort her life out for her. But maybe you should tell her you're worried about her, that we all are. You've got all this history, I'm sure she'll listen. There's nothing more we can do tonight anyway – short of gate-crashing that party.' She smiled at me and looked pointedly down at her slipper-clad feet. 'And I'm not really dressed for a night on the town.'

I woke up late the next day and still felt tired. I lay in bed for a long time, thinking. Dad had brought me tea, his way of saying, in the nicest possible way, it was about time I was up. I checked my email and read a sweet message from Jake – he'd got up early to write before they all went out and hit the slopes. He said the resort was cool and they were having a nice time so far, what they'd had of it, and that he was thinking of me. Then I showered and took my time getting dressed, knowing that when I was done I had to go and talk to Sally.

I knocked a few times on their front door and was just stepping back to look up at the house, thinking they must be out, when Sally's messy head appeared at her window and she waved feebly. She disappeared and I thought she'd come to the door, but instead the next noise I heard was the same window opening up. I stepped back again.

'Hey lady,' she croaked. 'I'm in bed still. Come up though,' and with that she threw her keys out at me and flopped back down out of sight. I let myself in and made two cups of tea before I headed up the stairs. Sally had managed to prop herself up as I pushed her door open.

'Hey. Oooh, you're amazing, thanks,' she said as she reached gleefully for her tea.

'You got home OK, then?'

'Oh, yeah, I crashed at Nadine's, and Ed drove me back this morning. I've been in bed since, I'm totally knackered. Mum wasn't best pleased; she's gone to the supermarket in a huff, I think. She'll be hours, I've never known anyone who could pass so much time happily just reading food labels . . . How was the rest of Anna's party?'

What was she talking about? 'I left about the same time as you, Sally. Mum was picking us up, remember?'

'Ohhh, sugar. Yeah, sorry about that, I kind of lost track of time. Are you cross with me?'

I stared into my tea for a second; confrontation wasn't my thing normally but I was cross with her and I wasn't going to lie about it.

'A bit.'

I looked up at her and she was rummaging through her bedside table drawer for lip balm. The fact she didn't seem to be listening emboldened me. If she didn't care if I was angry I might as well tell her.

'You never would have done that before you started hanging out with May and Nadine. Look, Sally, it's none of my business who you hang out with, but I'm worried . . . ' Sally was out of bed now, scraping back her tangle of hair and looking around the floor for jeans to throw on. 'You're so different. If it's just that you like hanging out with them, and if you genuinely like Ed, then that's great – but I'm worried that you're going out late to avoid thinking about your dad. I wish you'd talk to someone about it. Sally, you don't have to go through it on your own. If you can't talk to me I understand, it's family stuff, but I'd listen, any time. Or talk to Jake, please, don't bottle it all up, it's not good . . . '

'I will NOT talk to Jake.' Sally swung round from the wardrobe where she'd been looking for a jumper. Her face was screwed up with rage. I'd never seen her look like that, and my heart leaped in my chest as I realised how my good intentions had enraged her. 'And you'll keep quiet, do you get me?' She pointed a sharp finger at me, jabbing with her arm, almost as if she was mentally stabbing me. 'You. You think you know better than me what's going through my own head? You don't have a CLUE, with your perfect family and your perfect life – and your PERFECT boyfriend who you can't see is selfish and stubborn and just thinks of himself. And it IS none of your business who I hang out with. AND, if you must know, I AM thinking about Dad. You can't even imagine – I've found out exactly who that woman is and next time he goes on one of his "business trips" I'm going to find out where she lives, too, and I'm going to have it out with her and put an end to this thing before people find out . . . ' She'd gone back to looking through her wardrobe and was muttering to herself. It was so weird, sort of unhinged, like she'd forgotten her tirade at me the moment the words were out of her mouth, and now she was thinking about her crazy plan and it was like I wasn't there.

I had pain in my throat from forcing myself not to cry. I was shaking from the venom Sally had spat at me. I recognised nothing in the friend I thought I knew so well. I was out of my depth. I couldn't think of a thing to say and, even if I could, she needed to calm down before she'd hear anything, just as much as I needed to calm down before I said it.

I put down my unfinished tea, my fingers stiff with

tension from gripping the mug so hard. I tried to say I thought I'd better go, but no words would come out. So I slipped out of her bedroom silently, ran down the stairs, out of the front door, all the way to my front door, up my stairs, into my bedroom, and, as I shut the door behind me, all the tears I'd been holding on to flowed freely.

Chapter 10

♥

I t was freezing that week. When I left for college on Monday, everything was frosted. Hundreds of usually invisible spiders' webs had suddenly appeared in glittering strings and lattices of white. The pavements sparkled with the hint of ice.

I had to drive so slowly and carefully I was late for my first class and, as I got close to the door, I could hear they were watching some sort of film, so I decided instead of interrupting I'd wait in the library and join them after break. There was a lovely email from Jake when I logged on to a computer and opened my messages.

Hey gorgeous,

Still missing you, but having a great time - is that allowed? Our instructor is amazing (quite scary, so you have to do what he says or he looks like he might push your face in! It's really working though), and even if I do say so myself, I'm getting pretty darned good. You'd be impressed, honest! Was thinking, I should get back quite early on Sunday, and I'd planned

to hold on till Valentine's day on Wednesday,
but don't think I can wait (plus everywhere
will be packed out and I didn't book anything!)
so I thought maybe we could go out for dinner
Sunday night istead? What do you think? Can't
wait to see you. All my love, Jake. Xxx

I emailed back yes, and of course after that I was counting the hours even more impatiently until Sunday. By Wednesday we were snowed in. The parties had stopped and it seemed like everyone was hibernating – or starting to panic about work now term was in full swing. I took pictures of our white-covered village with Dad's digital camera and emailed them to Jake – boasting I could probably just pop out of the front door and go skiing myself. I missed him. But part of me was grateful he wasn't at home. Sally and I hadn't spoken since Sunday and I wasn't sure how I was going to explain it if we hadn't made some kind of reconciliation by the time he was back. Staying in touch just by email, with a good-night text now and then, made it easier not to let slip all that was going on. Over and over again, I imagined trying to explain to Jake all my worry for Sally without actually telling him the reason.

It was only a couple of months until study had to start in earnest for A-level exams, and, hard as I tried to get work done, I'd find myself staring at my notes, seeing nothing but Sally's angry face in my low moments, or Jake's welcome, smiling face in my better ones. I cheered myself by picturing his wind-blasted winter tan, and the romantic scene of the welcome-home meal we'd be having on Sunday night.

Sally wasn't the only one pulling the wool over her own eyes. I spent most of the week convincing myself that everything would be magically fixed when Jake came back. First, there'd be the most perfect romantic evening, then we'd have a whole week to spend with each other, because it was half-term and Jake had some extra days' holiday from work. I'd be over at their house all the time, and Sally and I would bump into each other in the kitchen, apologies would come pouring out, we'd hug, and everything would start to heal. I'd made myself believe that this fiction would become reality and by Saturday night I was excited and happy – and impatient to be waking up the next, glorious morning.

I woke up late again, after taking so long to fall asleep in my excitement, and after brunch I warned Mum and Dad the bathroom was mine for at least two hours. I had the longest bath, gave myself a pedicure and manicure, moisturised to within an inch of saturation and put on my favourite perfume.

By five-thirty I'd perfected my make-up and was straightening my hair when my phone rang – the ringtone that meant it was Jake! I was so excited I couldn't stifle a little squeal. But as soon as the words 'Hey, you,' were out of my mouth, I knew from the quiet on the other end of the phone that something wasn't going according to plan.

'Hey you too.' Jake sounded loving but sort of sad. 'How are you?'

I wanted to say, 'Excited. So happy you're home, I can't wait another half an hour, come over now ' but all I could say was, 'Good, thanks. How are you?'

'I'm OK. But listen, I'm so, so sorry but I need to cancel tonight. There's nothing I want more than to go to dinner with you, but there's some stuff going on here and Mum needs me . . . I'm so sorry, Erica, I promise we'll see each other tomorrow . . . '

My heart fell through the floor. Although I knew he must be telling the truth, little demons inside my head were telling me he'd somehow decided, on the flight home, that he didn't love me at all. He'd finally realised he could do better and was trying to let me down gently. I told myself off for being so self-obsessed and tried to think how hard it must be for him.

'Don't worry. It's OK, I understand. But what's

happened, Jake? Please tell me what's going on.'

'I can't really talk now, I'll explain tomorrow. I'll call you as soon as I can in the morning, I promise, OK?'

I think I said OK back, I can't really remember. I do remember unplugging my irons on autopilot, half my hair still a wavy mess, and curling up on my bed, incapacitated by disappointment.

After about two hours Mum must have guessed what had happened. There was the faintest knock at my door and her face slowly peered in at me. She crept in, wrapped me up in her arms and asked if I'd come down and have some food with her and Dad, she knew it wasn't the same but they'd love it if I joined them.

'I'll be down in a minute,' I said dimly, trying to smile.

She nodded, brushing a strand of hair away from my face, and left me alone while I tied my half-done hair back out of the way and pep-talked myself. You'll see Jake tomorrow, I thought. Don't be a baby just because things didn't go exactly how you'd imagined in your funny little head. You just need to wait for things to calm down and it'll all be fine.

After a quiet dinner in front of the TV, Dad went to bed with a book just after ten and Mum stayed up with me and we watched a film. It was just before midnight when my phone rang. Mum reached for the remote to turn the TV down, but I jumped up and rushed into the kitchen. I couldn't have guessed what he'd say but I didn't know if it might be private.

'Hey,' I answered, as gently as I could, and quietly because I knew Dad would be asleep upstairs.

'I didn't wake you, did I?' asked Jake. I said no of course he hadn't, but he was already talking over me. 'Sally's gone. She had a massive row with Mum after she stayed out all night again last night. I shouldn't have got involved, but she was really going off at Mum and it wasn't fair – I guess we sort of ganged up on her.' I could hear the guilt in his voice, but it was quickly replaced with urgent worry. 'We were going to go out to look for her just now, but she's taken the car. Erica, do you have numbers for May or Ed or any of that lot? We tried the number we had for Nadine, but it's disconnected. We don't know what to do – the police don't want to know yet, she has to be missing longer before they can help.'

But I didn't have any of the numbers he needed. 'I'm so sorry, Jake, I don't. I don't know any of them well enough really, I'm pretty sure Ruth and Charlotte won't either, but I can try Anna. Have you tried Rich – he'll have a number for Munch, won't he? He might know something?'

'Of course he will – I'm such an idiot, thanks. I'll call

him now. Can you try Anna in the meantime and let me know? Thanks, Erica.' He hung up. I scrolled straight down my address book and called Anna. No answer, and I knew she wouldn't have credit to pick up voicemails so I texted.

Hi, it's Erica. Sal's missing! Do u have nos for Ed, Munch or May? Let me no. x

I pressed 'Send' and it was then I realised I probably had a better idea where Sally had gone than any of those people. Dazed by the panicked whirl of thoughts in my head, I walked back into the living room, quietly closing the door. I must have had quite a look on my face because Mum got straight up and came over to me.

'Sally's gone,' I said.

'What do you mean?' Mum frowned.

'She's taken the car. They don't know where . . . ' A sob escaped from me, my knees gave way and I sank to the floor. Mum crouched beside me and held me.

'She'll be OK, darling, she's not stupid . . . '

'Mum,' I interrupted her, 'I think I know where she's gone – at least, I don't know where, but I think I know what's she's doing.' It all came flooding out then, the visit to her dad's office, the secret I was sworn to keep and the reason Sally had gone off the rails. I remembered the anger in her face, and the way she'd seemed almost insane when I saw her last, and I was terrified of where she might be and what might have happened. I was horrified that it could be my fault. Why hadn't I kept trying to convince her? I was so selfish, thinking of how hurt I'd been, instead of how she needed help.

When I'd finished, the relief I'd imagined feeling when the secret was finally out didn't come. I just felt guilty and ashamed. Mum took charge then. She said we had to go right over to see Steph and tell them what I knew, and we could drive them wherever they needed to go to find her. I was in some kind of disabling shock. She practically had to put my coat on for me and push me out of the door.

Chapter 11

♥

'I thought you might need the use of my car,' said Mum when Jake opened the door. His face was grey and drawn and tense.

'Great! We were just talking about taxis – thanks, come in,' said Jake, leaving us to follow as he rushed in to his mum. Steph had clearly been crying, but the news that they had a car and could go out and start searching got her up and grabbing her shoes.

'Before we go, Steph, I think there may be more to this than just driving into town and trying the nightclubs and friends' houses.' Mum looked at me. 'Are you going to tell them, or should I?' Steph was poised, one arm in her coat, keys in hand. Jake was bent over his trainers on the sofa, lacing up. He looked up at me and I looked back.

'I think she might have gone after your dad.' I stared down at the floor then, so I don't know what their reactions were. Mum must have got the idea I might say something wrong because she took over.

'Sally's got the idea, somehow, that Simon's been

having an affair. She told Erica, the last time they saw each other, that when he went off on his next business trip she was going to confront this woman that she thinks he's been seeing. I assume you called Simon when you knew she'd gone, but it might be worth letting him know she could be on the way to his hotel.'

Steph spoke then, quietly, but with the most dignity I've witnessed in my life so far I think.

'Faye, it's very good and wonderfully diplomatic of you to talk as if it's some fantasy Sally has concocted, but she's not stupid, and neither am I. I suppose we shouldn't have kept sweeping it under the carpet for all this time. Let's get in the car, if that's OK, and I'll call Simon as we drive – hopefully, if Erica is right, Sally will be with him by now.'

We made for the door and I watched Jake lay the gentlest, supportive hand on his mum's shoulder as she walked ahead of him, but his face was straining, as if his jaw was clenched so hard all his teeth might fracture under the pressure. He stared determinedly ahead. I wasn't there to him.

The front door was about to slam behind us as we rushed out into the frozen night air, when a shrill alarm sounded, shooting through me like a knife and making me jump. The landline was going. Steph threw herself back into the house and grabbed the receiver.

'Hello? Yes, this is she . . . ' A shaking hand raised to her mouth and, as she squeezed her eyes shut tight, her face crumpled and a tear caught the light from the porch. We all held our breath. 'Is she OK? . . . Yes, I see. We'll be there in fifteen minutes. Thank you.' She gasped in a breath with a shudder as she gently dropped the receiver back into place.

'There was an accident, a crash – she's OK, well, no, she's hurt – Faye, could you take us to the hospital?' I felt my heart stop in my chest and the breath run completely out of me.

'Of course,' Mum said, but before we could move I felt a jolt of pain in my arm and I think I let out a yelp. I turned to see Jake had grabbed my arm.

'You KNEW!' His voice cracked in a strange growl. His face was so full of pain, there were tears in his eyes, those eyes I loved so much. I wanted to hold him, to say sorry, but he hated me with every inch, I could see it clearly in his face and it terrified me. I felt cold and clammy. He shook me and pain shot through my arm. 'You knew, and you said NOTHING! She could be dying . . .'

'JAKE!' Steph screamed, crying like I was, like Jake was. 'That's ENOUGH!' I felt Jake release me and

Mum's arm was round me, holding me up, holding me together. 'We can't run through every "if" and "but". Let's just get to the hospital. *Please.*'

That drive to hospital was the worst fifteen minutes of my life. I sobbed the whole way, trying to stay silent, staring out of the window so Jake wouldn't see me and think I had no right to cry over what I'd caused. I huddled as small as I could make myself in the corner of the back seat, wanting to disappear. I didn't turn to look at him, I didn't dare. I could see his livid, glowering hatred every time I closed my eyes. Most of all, I dreaded finding Sally bloody and badly hurt – or worse. How could this night – that I'd been wishing would arrive – have ended like this? The world was crumbling under my feet.

Chapter 12

♥

I felt nauseous as we pulled into the car park, and it wasn't just the sickly, chemical glow of the hospital lighting bleeding out into the murky night. Part of me wanted to rush into the hospital and find Sally, another part of me dreaded seeing her. I felt ashamed and frightened and so I hung back as the others rushed into reception.

It was chaos inside. Clearly a lot of drunken nights out had ended here, and I imagined how depressed it must make the staff, having to clear up the mess everyone had got themselves into. But I was thankful for all the noise and rushing people – it meant fewer eyes were on me.

Mum stayed in the background with me as we followed Steph and Jake through to the cubicle where Sally was being treated. Mum was practically dragging me along. My hand was over my mouth as I got a glimpse of Sally. She was awake, thank goodness. There was a brace around her neck and a large, vicious cut on her head, which had been cleaned and stitched but still looked terrifying. It ran from near her hairline right down through her eyebrow and scarily close to her eye. Steph let out a little cry and rushed over, obviously wanting to scoop Sally up in her arms but holding herself back for fear of hurting her, she was so battered and bruised.

I think Sally saw me and gave the slightest smile. But it seemed right to leave the family alone together. We waited back at reception to hear more news. Mum had gone to get us some hideous machine tea, just for sake of something to do I think, when I saw Simon arrive. His face gave little away. I saw him have an exchange with a receptionist, who gestured for him to go through to the cubicle. I watched him disappear in the direction we'd just come from. I stared after him, into the corridor, wondering what Sally's reaction would be when she saw him, or Steph's. Or Jake's. Hopelessness rushed through me again as I thought of Jake, but I had no energy left for tears.

Then Steph reappeared and I watched her scan the waiting area. I thought she saw me, although she made no move to come over. Perfect in her timing as always, Mum emerged, plastic drinks in hand, and she and Steph spoke. Mum just listened and nodded as Steph spoke and gesticulated shakily for what felt like a very long time, then she said something back. I could see she was worried. She leaned in towards Steph to force her to make eye contact. Steph's hand came up to her face again and she seemed to cry for a moment. Mum did her best to give her a comforting hug while balancing the drinks, and then they exchanged a few more words, nodding with each other, Mum seeming to wait for reassurance Steph would be OK. When she got it, they parted and I watched as she came back over to where I was sitting.

Another driver at the scene of the accident had told the police what had happened. Sally had tried to overtake at the wrong moment. She'd realised her mistake but had left it too late to get back in lane and had veered off the opposite side of the road – and into a tree. Thank goodness the other driver had managed to break in time and wasn't hit or hurt. Thank goodness Sally hadn't been going faster. Thank goodness she'd had her seatbelt on . . . She had a broken leg, a fracture in her wrist, whiplash, and the cut on her head. She had no internal bleeding that they could tell but, because she'd hit her head, she would have to stay in hospital for a day or two so they could keep an eye on her. Mum explained that Steph had said we shouldn't wait because they didn't know how long they'd be – and besides Simon had his car there now. I just nodded. Mum gave me a hug and then we left, abandoning our teas untouched.

I'd like to say I didn't sleep a wink that night. You might think I didn't deserve to. But after Dad forced a cocoa on me, I virtually crawled up to my bed, exhausted. I was drained and numb but sleep was a blessed escape. I remember thinking I didn't care how long I slept for, even that I didn't really care if I ever woke up.

Chapter 13

♥

I came round confused. I could hear clanging and thudding in the kitchen, and voices – the TV on in the living room. But it was dark in my room. The streaks of daylight that would usually sneak through the blind, even on grey days, weren't there – was it still night? We hadn't got home until the early hours, so it couldn't be, and besides there wouldn't be cooking noises. It must be evening. What day was it? Monday? Had I slept for days? Maybe Mum and Dad were just letting me sleep.

It took a few minutes for all the details of Sunday night to come back to me, and each new detail was like another weight on me. Sally's blood and bruises, that horrific cut on her face. Simon arriving at the hospital, Steph leaning on Mum, overwhelmed by all that was happening. Jake's hand crushing my arm in hate, his pain and rage-filled eyes. It didn't have to be real. All the noises of life I could hear in the house, if I could just ignore them and stay where I was, cocooned in darkness and in my duvet and in sleep – none of these things that had happened had to be real if I could just hide.

The phone rang downstairs and I heard Mum's voice, but the conversation was muffled and I couldn't make out any words. Once the cordless receiver had bleeped back into place though, I could hear her coming up the stairs. She stopped outside my door, did one of her gentle knocks and slowly eased the door open. I didn't move, but I didn't pretend to be asleep. She sat down by the head of my bed.

'How you feeling, hon?' I shrugged slightly. 'Steph just called. Sally's doing well, she's going to be just fine. In fact, they think she'll be coming home tomorrow. But Steph wondered if you might like to see her tonight – visiting hours at the hospital are six till eight. They're popping in at six but, if you'd like to speak to her on your own, you'd have her to yourself from about half past. It's up to you, darling, but if you wanted to go we'd need to leave in about forty-five minutes. I'll be ready to drive you if you want a lift but you'll need to get up and showered. I'll leave you to decide.'

Bless Mum for knowing I couldn't have stood any pressure just then, and that I wouldn't want to drive to the hospital on my own. But of course I had to go and see Sally. She might hate me for telling her secret. She might blame me for not forcing her to tell it herself, just like Jake. But I had to know, and I wanted to see that she was OK, before she came home, so I could avoid seeing Jake.

In the car, I wondered if Steph had tipped me off on the visiting hours because Jake had said he didn't want me coming to the house. I didn't know if I was being paranoid. At least I could assume Sally wanted to see me, or at least hadn't said she didn't want to, or Steph wouldn't have suggested it.

'How did Steph sound?' I asked Mum. She looked confused. 'On the phone, did she sound angry? Do you think she blames me?' I stared into my lap.

'Listen to me, Erica.' Mum's voice was almost stern. 'You couldn't have stopped this. Sally's got a mind of her own, you can't take responsibility for her, it's too much. Yes, she asked you to keep a dangerous secret as it turns out, but you did what you thought was right at the time. That's all any of us can do.'

Even though she's my mum and I knew she'd say whatever made me feel better, I believed her, and I did feel a little better. By the time we reached the hospital I was looking forward to seeing Sally. There were things I wanted to know about the past couple of months that I hoped she might be able to tell me. When I peeked through the curtain, Sally was sitting up. There was a little TV on an arm coming out of the wall and it was on quietly, but she didn't seem to be watching really.

'Hey.' She smiled when she saw me. 'Come in. I'm sooo bored.'

I smiled back and walked round the bed to sit down. I tried not to stare at the stitched cut on her face, but it still looked angry and painful and I obviously didn't hide my shock too well. Her fingers reached up and touched the cut gingerly.

'The doctors say I'll probably be scarred for life.'

I tried harder to hide my feelings this time and leaned in to whisper to her. 'Doctors pretend like they know everything, but they're wrong sometimes, you know. It'll heal. You'll still be beautiful.'

She shook her head but smiled again for a moment, then the sadness came back.

'Did you see Dad last night?' I nodded. 'He's moving out . . .' I bowed my head. Everything she hadn't wanted to happen was happening and I felt like it was all my fault and, after all the agonising, there hadn't been any point in me betraying her secret in the end – by the time Mum and I had turned up at their house, Sally had already crashed.

'I'm so sorry, Sally.' My voice was shaking. 'When no one knew where you were . . . I thought I was helping . . . telling, I mean.'

She shook her head. 'I know I put you in a difficult place, Erica, I'm sorry. Don't worry about it. It's weird – this is what I was dreading. I imagined it would be the end of my world – but I had a long chat with Mum and she sort of seems actually happier. Sort of . . . stronger than I've known her for a long time.'

I remembered Steph's reaction at the house on Sunday and knew exactly what she meant. 'And I wasn't being fair to her, believing Jake meant more to her . . . ' Sally turned to me and shook her head again. 'You know, she knew. She knew about Dad, so it wasn't really a secret anyway, after everything. There was me thinking I was so clever and important.' She laughed humourlessly and laid back and closed her eyes for a moment. She looked tired, and I thought of Mum waiting outside so I stood up.

'I should probably leave you to sleep, you look tired.' But she reached out to me with her plaster-encased hand.

'No, wait.' I stayed standing. 'It's funny how a good smack to the head and incarceration in a hospital bed can clear your thoughts . . . You were right, you know, about me ignoring things. Nadine and Ed and Munch, even May – they're not real friends, not like you. I'm sorry for the way I was.'

'Don't be silly.' I laughed it off. But secretly I felt happy and relieved that she said it.

'You'll come and see me, won't you? I'm going to be an invalid, stuck in my house for ever. You'll come over and watch movies with me?' I sat down then. She said that like it was so simple.

'I don't know Sally, I want to. But Jake hates me. Really, you should have seen him when we heard you'd been hurt. And I'm not sure your mum's my biggest fan either . . . I just don't think I'd be welcome.'

Sally rolled her eyes. 'Erica, Mum loves you, she always has. She wouldn't have suggested you come and see me if she blamed you for anything, would she? Believe me, it's me she blames. I'm going to have to be on my best behaviour for at least a year to get back in her good books. And Jake – what did I tell you about him? He thinks he knows better than anyone, he's a stubborn pain in the bee-hind. But last night was last night and he listens to Mum. And he loves you too. You know that, come on. I've never seen him so gooey as he's been the past few months. He'll come round. All the more reason you should spend lots of time at ours, being lovely at him!' She fake-grinned at me, acknowledging her pure selfishness in trying to persuade me, and I felt good as we waved each other goodbye, sort of like I'd got my friend back.

I even let myself believe maybe she was right about

Jake, too, that he'd come round and, when I thought of him on the way home, I saw him smiling at me again. Instead of remembering his anger, when I closed my eyes, I felt him sweeping me up in a hug, the warm skin of his cheek brushing mine like that first time on our bench.

Chapter 14

♥

I nbox (1). The next day there was a fresh new white line at the top of my email messages – from Jake! I clicked on it before I'd even thought about what it might say.

Hi Erica,

I'm sorry not to say this to you in person, I know I should, but it's too hard to even think about seeing you. I think it's best that we don't see each other any more.

I don't think I'll ever be able to forgive you for the secret you kept. We'll never know whether Sally's accident would have happened if things had been different and out in the open, but the point is, you kept a secret about my own family from me, one that belonged to me at least as much as to you. I thought we were always honest with each other and I can't be with someone who can keep such huge secrets so easily. I'm sorry things had to finish this way, but I think you can understand.

Jake.

My heart was lurching, over and over. I thought I might throw up. I was filled with that horror you get when you've smashed something precious and you're just coming to the realisation of what you've done, before you start to wish with every atom of yourself that you could turn back time, because just a few moments ago you lived in happy oblivion of this moment when all was lost. Did he really mean he didn't want to see me any more – ever?

When I thought of all the happiness I'd had with Jake, I felt a physical pain like it was being ripped away. I felt heavy and breathless as I mechanically closed my email and shut down. I rushed to my room, closed the door behind me, collapsed against it and cried and cried until I was exhausted. I couldn't move and I don't know how long it was until I managed to drag myself into my bed to hide in the folds of my duvet – one hour? Two? Then I slept. It was my only escape from a world where Jake hated me.

Mum left food by my bed when I wouldn't come down for dinner or tell her why, but I didn't eat it. The next day she insisted I'd feel better if I got up, but I walked round in a daze. Occasionally I'd venture downstairs and slump in front of the TV. But of course the day after I got that email, it was Valentine's day and every stupid programme seemed to be about love. Invisible rays of schmaltz would shoot out of the TV and pierce my heart, making me think of Jake and sending me back to my bed in tears. All I could think about was that I couldn't stand him being angry with me. I lived like a hermit, ignoring any texts or calls I got from friends or, when they persisted, sending back the shortest answers I could get away with.

Jake's email had made me feel so small and worthless, I was too scared to read it again, let alone think about replying. But by Saturday the return to college was looming. I knew I couldn't pretend this horribleness wasn't happening. I'd have to face seeing everyone and if I wasn't my normal self – and if I didn't mention Jake in every other sentence – there would be questions. I had to pull myself together and try to fix my life. So I made a strong cup of tea, switched on the computer and prepared to feel the force of the blow again. What could I say to him to make him understand?

But a funny thing happened. Despite how prepared I'd been to explain how sorry I was, how hard it had been for me and how I could understand how angry he was, when I read his words again, I didn't feel sorry.

He hinted he still blamed me for what happened to Sally, but he didn't have the guts to say it openly, even in an email, let alone to my face. He said I'd kept a secret that was more his than mine, well, that wasn't true: it was Sally's and she had asked me to keep it. I'm sure if it had been him who had asked me, he would have expected me to keep it too. But the thing that really filled me with anger – indignant, strengthening anger – was that one phrase: *I can't be with someone who can keep such huge secrets so easily.* Easily?! How dare he think it had been easy? The anguish I'd been through! That one statement made me realise he hadn't spent the slightest bit of effort to imagine my side of things. He was thinking of himself. And the sign-off: *I think you can understand.* Not *I hope you can understand,* but a self-important *I* think *you can understand.*

All the moral certainty I had thought made Jake so strong and amazing now seemed more like self-righteous stubbornness – and laziness in not trying to see other people's points of view. Maybe I was being too hard on him. Maybe I was being defensive because I did still wonder if I could have saved Sally from her accident if I'd handled things differently. But if Sally could forgive me, why couldn't Jake even try?

There wasn't a single mention in the email of his anger towards me on that Sunday night, either. Not that I didn't understand completely that he'd been terrified and worried at that moment. But I was terrified too and it was truly horrible the way he'd looked at me, and gripped me so hard he'd left bruises. There was no way he could know that, and maybe he didn't even remember, but his ferocity had really frightened me and I thought maybe he might just mention it.

What was the use of me apologising again and again if he wasn't prepared to listen and understand my reasons? He'd already decided that he wouldn't be able to forgive me. I was torn between my anger at his words and wanting to reach out and try to explain my side of the story. So I decided that I wouldn't reply just then. Deciding to wait until I was sure what to say, even though I knew that meant I'd risk losing Jake for ever, felt a little bit like choosing myself, my dignity, over him. And it wasn't easy. I'd leave it at that, and maybe we'd be over. It hurt all over again to think about it. Part of me couldn't believe I was choosing not to reach out to at least try and fix this. But the other part of me knew I had to be true to myself first, even if it meant everything Jake and I'd had would be lost.

Chapter 15

♥

Sally and I emailed or messaged each other almost every day. I kept notes for her in Media studies and nagged her classmates in her other subjects to do the same, until she eventually came back to college to a loving welcome from everyone. Ruth threw a 'comeback' party and this time Sally stayed until the end and we came home together.

Spring sprung. The world came out of hibernation and there was all this energy and colour and sunshine. The earth was turning and time was moving on without me, like a missed bus disappearing down the road. The evenings got longer and warmer and Charlotte and Ruth would invite me into town after class, but I'd smile and say no thanks and that I was going home to revise. I worked hard, right through Easter and into our final term. I'll admit my motives weren't entirely noble – studying kept my mind occupied and if I'd tried to go out and have fun I just would have felt Jake's absence more sharply. So instead I sat at home and imagined sitting in the park with them, seeing Jake arrive through the gates and come over, smiling, to wind his arm round my waist and squeeze hello . . .

So many things made me think of him, and every time he came into my mind I thought about replying to that email. But the once or twice I was brave enough to get as far as just reading it again, I felt the anger still inside me. I didn't want to send an angry reply. It was heartbreaking enough we weren't seeing or speaking to each other. The only thing that could be worse was if we started to hate each other too. So I kept putting it off. I forced myself to think about my work and my future. But Jake had been the voice in my head that spurred me on when I was finding a subject hard or was cross with myself for getting stuck with an essay. Now I had to shut that voice out, because it was angry and accusing. Some days I cried over my desk, feeling like I was only half a person without him and all the strength he'd given me.

The exams were going to happen whether I was ready or not, and whether Jake was there to get me through them or not, and I'd given up so much of my social life to study that actually, in the end, they went well. Except I had one on my birthday, which was a bit rubbish. Sally and Ruth and I had a few afternoon drinks in a pub garden in town to celebrate. I'd been offered a place at

Brighton to do fashion and business, provided I got the grades, so it should have been a double celebration really, but we all either had an exam the next day, or one the day after so no one was up for a big night out. In a way, I was glad. It stopped me thinking about how different the summer, and my birthday, might have been if I'd still been with Jake – well, it stopped me thinking about it *much* anyway. That morning, I'd come down to breakfast to find presents from my family laid out on the dining table as per tradition. I still felt the excitement of seeing the mysterious, wrapped shapes, all for me. But they reminded me of Jake's Christmas stocking and the love that had gone into each beautifully romantic gift.

Sitting there in that pub garden, the sun shining on the colours of the flowers, and warming our skin, the birds singing gently, I should have felt that rush of summer happiness and anticipation. Instead I felt the space on the bench next to me where I wanted Jake to be.

We did a pretty good job of avoiding each other, Jake and I. I saw Sally all the time at college and we met up for extended study breaks at Coco's, so I didn't have to go over to her house, which was better anyway because we'd talk quite a bit about her parents.

Sally's dad had rented a flat in London and she was actually looking forward to being able to visit a couple of weekends a month. She said she liked the glamour of essentially having a crash pad in London when she fancied it. I know things were hard for her and she joked to cover things up a bit, but she did admit that, even though her parents had been careful about discussing things in front of her, her dad had been a wreck. She'd never seen him like that before. He'd promised never to see the other woman again – Veronica her name turned out to be – and begged Steph to have him back. But she wouldn't. I worried when Sally told me that, thinking she might be angry at Steph for letting the family break up, but actually I think when her dad had fallen off his pedestal it gave her new perspective. She and Steph had been spending a lot of time together, just the two of them, talking properly about the split, and how Sally had been feeling about things, and she seemed genuinely at peace with the situation.

One particularly warm day in July, after the exams were over, Sally told me, over a Coco's special double-choc ice-cream shake, that Steph had dropped a bombshell. She was moving to Scotland to live with her sister in Falkirk for a while. So after a brief freak-out Sally had decided she wanted to get into Glasgow to do law, so they wouldn't be too far apart after all. And, she said, Jake was thinking he'd finally be able to take up his deferred place to do an art degree in Edinburgh, now she and Steph might both be headed up to Scotland anyway. I nodded politely and stared into my drink, hoping the conversation would move on quickly. But Sally was testing me.

'You two haven't even spoken since the accident, have you? I can't understand it, you were so close before and you haven't even tried to make up.'

I felt a twinge of irritation at her then. She seemed to have no idea how she'd changed things between me and Jake. It was her who had caused all this, in a way. But I couldn't blame her after the tough time she'd been through. I took a breath in and let the tension go.

'We didn't need to talk for him to make his feelings pretty clear, Sal. Too much changed between us . . . ' I held myself back from going into the details – I didn't want to start talking about it, it was too hard. 'You know how it is,' I shrugged, remembering that December day on the platform at the station, when we'd talked about her break-up with Mark. 'It's all for the best.'

She shook her head sadly. 'Jake still mopes about it you know. It just seems sad, to throw that all away, just because you're both so stubborn.'

I felt a flutter in my chest when she said that. He was still thinking about me too? But then she let it go, and started talking about this guy Ruth had apparently started seeing. She'd heard it was getting all hot and heavy and he was going to follow her to Leeds when she took up her university place there.

We finished our drinks and Sally went off to meet her mum. As I drove home I thought about what she'd said. Jake wasn't over me. Maybe she was right and we'd both just been too stubborn. She made me realise how obvious it had been that we were right for each other – people had seen us as this great couple. But I had to bury the feelings she'd stirred up. For my own sanity I'd had to stop myself reading over that damned email. It had taken five months of serious distraction tactics to avoid confronting him. But I found myself wondering what would have happened if it had just been worded a bit differently, or I'd swallowed my pride and replied with a calm explanation. I turned the radio on loudly, found a song to sing along to, and tried my best to shake the thoughts from my head.

When I got home I decided I'd have a clear-out and makeover my room. So for a few days I busied myself fillling bags full of stuff to take to charity shops and trying out paint testers. One Monday, I thought I'd try moving my furniture. I plugged my iPod into the stereo and put on my most upbeat playlist, as loud as I thought

I could get away with. I threw open my bedroom window and propped open my door to let the air through, scraped my hair back into a knot to keep it out of the way, and proceeded to spring clean (or summer clean, I guess, if there is such a thing).

But, as the third track faded out, I heard a loud banging at the door that made me jump. I hesitated, knowing I should hurry because whoever it was may have been knocking for a while, drowned out by the music, while thinking at this time of day, in the middle of the afternoon, it was likely to be someone selling something, dishcloths or religion or whatever. Manners got the better of me though and I put the music on pause, skipped down the stairs in my bare feet and swung open the door.

And there was Jake. Seeing him standing there was sort of like being punched in the chest – I actually felt winded. His hands were jammed awkwardly in his pockets and he had an odd expression on, like he was trying to smile through his nervous frown but didn't know if smiling was appropriate.

'Hi,' he said. He looked incredible. I mean he just had on torn old jeans and an even older, faded T-shirt and flip-flops. But he had that easy summer tan already and the tension in his arms squared those amazing shoulders.

In body, he was this beautiful person I still loved, the same face, lips, hands, hair, skin. My instinct was to reach out to touch him. I wanted to hold him and have him hold me, to snake my hand around his torso and feel his warm, strong frame supporting me. I had to fight against the will in my muscles because it wasn't allowed. I don't know how to describe it, there was this barrier – I suppose it was like he was on the other side of a thick glass wall that we'd constructed between us. I don't know how long I just stood there, lost for words.

'Um, I'm driving up to Falkirk with Mum tomorrow – did Sally tell you?' I nodded to let him know I knew his plans, or at least some of them. 'And I have a meeting at the university on Monday and then I need to look around for flat shares and stuff, so I'm staying with my aunt for a bit and I don't know if I'll be back down before . . . well, I don't know if I'll be back – we've already had an offer on the house . . . ' He looked up the street for a moment, as if he'd surprised even himself with the realisation he was really leaving for good. 'So anyway, I thought I'd better say goodbye, I mean I *wanted* to say goodbye.' He frowned deeply and looked away, and I realised I must be staring, and that it must be really difficult for him standing there, explaining his presence.

I couldn't face asking him in though. It was awkward

enough standing on the doorstep with a metre between us, the thought of standing in the kitchen with tea, or sitting on the sofa – it was too much.

'Wow, big changes,' I said, trying to keep the conversation friendly. 'Erm, I was going to walk up to the shop actually – we need milk. It's such a nice day, do you want to walk with me? We could take a detour via the rec or something.'

'Sure,' he nodded.

'Gimme a sec, I'll just put some shoes on.' I left him kicking his feet outside for a couple of minutes while I grabbed some flip-flops, checked the mirror and then wondered why; it wasn't like we were on a date. I switched off the stereo, shut and locked the window, and took a deep breath.

My blood was racing with the excitement of seeing Jake and with the uncertainty of what we'd say to each other. But he'd come to say goodbye. Soon someone else would be living in his house. All the drawings would come down off his walls, all the memories painted over by intruders . . .

I allowed myself a couple of seconds and then headed back down, grabbing my keys on the way out, and my wallet, so he didn't twig that the needing milk story was made up.

'Sally says you're off to Brighton then?' Jake started

off the small talk as we walked slowly. I pulled at strands of my hair, not knowing what to do with my hands and thinking it must be frizzy from being tied back.

'Yeah, as long as I get the grades. So we'd be headed in opposite directions then I guess; you guys North, me South,' I added needlessly. I was desperate to keep talking, about anything, the more boring and less emotional the better. 'It'll be nice you're all nearish to each other still, what with Sally going to Glasgow. Edinburgh will be a great place to be, I reckon. It's really pretty and I bet there's loads of great places to go out.'

We got to the top of the road and I turned down a footpath without thinking then regretted it, because it felt so intimate – a cosy, secret little tunnel cocooned by trees. We had to squash up close to walk and keep talking and I felt Jake's arm brush against mine. It gave me goosebumps.

'Brighton should be fun, too – there's a great music scene, you'll love it.'

I held up my hand to halt him. 'If I get the grades, remember!' I laughed nervously. 'I'm not there yet!'

'You'll get the grades,' Jake said quietly.

Oh. He still believed in me. His soft, sure tone was like a hand reaching into my chest to touch my heart. I was suddenly enveloped in my memories. That feeling I'd had when we were together, of being loved and trusted and believed in, strong and whole, came back to me in a rush. I stopped walking and breathed deliberately, trying to hold myself together. Letting Jake go would be like losing a part of myself, letting it die – did I really have to do it? What if I held on to him now and didn't ever let go? I could visit him in Scotland, and he could come down to Brighton for gigs. Everything new we were going to discover, all the new friends we'd make, we could do it all together as a couple and be happy and complete.

I looked up from the floor and I was gazing into Jake's eyes. Our faces were just a few centimetres apart. I wanted to touch him and kiss him but we were both frozen, looking at each other, not knowing what to say. I wished I knew what he was thinking.

'You never replied to my email . . . you got it, right? I was hoping to hear something back.'

My heart was thumping so wildly I thought I might pass out. He hadn't meant it when he said he didn't want to see me! He just wanted a reply. What had I done, ignoring his plea to talk about what had happened? Had I thrown away what could have been the happiest summer of my life?

'Yes, I got it, I'm sorry.' It seemed ridiculous now that I hadn't replied and I didn't know how to explain. 'I didn't think there was much I could say – it felt like you'd made your mind up.' I tried not to sound too shaky.

'Really?' Jake went quiet for a moment.

I wanted him to say that of course he hadn't made his mind up, he was wrong, he missed me, he wanted me back. I wanted him to lift me up and love me again.

'I was sort of hoping you would reply, though. I thought you might want to explain, apologise . . . '

Apologise? All the wishing and wanting in my head screeched to a halt like a needle tearing across a record snatched from its turntable. I remembered the anger I'd felt when I read that email and found it rising in me again. I had to fight against it with all the calm I could muster. Jake's eyes were searching my face and I wondered if he registered the change in me: it felt too huge to go unnoticed. There we were, head to head on this footpath where we'd been many times before in quite different circumstances. I wanted to go back in time to when I'd just felt love, instead of this swirling, overpowering mix of frustration and hurt and longing.

'Did you ever think how hard it was for me?' I tried to keep my words slow and quiet and questioning, but my voice was cracked and wobbly. 'Can't you imagine how hard it was for me to do what Sally asked me to do? How I wanted to tell you every minute we were together the one thing she'd begged me not to?' It was impossible to

hide my emotion. I was quaking. It was all I could do not
to cry. 'That night, New Year's Eve, I started to tell you
– you didn't understand what I was saying but I hated
hiding it from you, I wanted to let it all out.'

'Then why didn't you?' Jake's voice was tensing too.
'You could have, you should have, it wasn't your secret
to keep.' I remembered then, that he'd said that in his
email, too. It just wasn't fair.

'That's not true, Jake, it's just not.' I felt the tears
welling in my chest and crumpling my face, when a man
walking his dog appeared round the bend in the footpath
and my sentence trailed off. We had to press ourselves
right up against the trees to let him through and, seeing
my chance to regain my dignity, I followed him out of
the lane as swiftly as I could, passing Jake and heading
back out on to the pavement.

I kept walking briskly to the little green a few metres
away where we could sit down on the bench there. I
didn't look back but I could sense Jake following. I
reached the bench and sat on the edge, staring down at
my hands, and I waited for Jake to sit down too.

'You said in your email that the secret I kept was more
yours than mine, but it doesn't work like that.' I couldn't
look at Jake; I knew if I looked at him, his face would
scramble my brain and I'd melt. As much as I wanted to

melt, I didn't want to give in, either. I needed to make him see he was wrong. I needed him to realise he wasn't being fair. 'It's like saying – well, say you painted a picture of that house.' I gestured across the green. 'You wouldn't say the painting then belongs to the house, or even the owners of the house. It doesn't work, because a secret doesn't belong to the content of itself, it belongs to the person who knows it, like a painting belongs to the person who paints it, not to the person or thing depicted in it. It was Sally's secret. She was my best friend and she asked me to keep it. You can't honestly think it was easy for me to do that?'

I looked at Jake then. He was staring at me but I couldn't read his expression. It was thoughtful and intense and could have meant he was realising his mistake, but equally it could have shown he was just waiting for me to finish before he tried to shoot down my argument. Too scared to find out which was true, I kept talking.

'I wanted her to tell you what she was going through, I told her you'd understand, that you'd be the one person who really could. But she was adamant you were the last person I should tell.' I realised, as I couldn't hold the tears back any longer, that I was in danger of bringing Sally's motives into the argument, and that wasn't fair. Blaming her wasn't what I wanted to do. 'Anyway, if you really think it was easy for me, you never knew me at all. That's why I didn't reply.' I turned away, trying to hide my sobs.

'You're right, Erica, I shouldn't have thought it was easy for you.'

That flutter was back in my chest when he sounded sorry. I let myself look at him, still hoping that somehow there could be a happy ending to this. It felt like an eternity waiting for his next sentence – I imagined him saying he'd been wrong, he was so sorry, the summer wasn't the same without me, Sally had been right to forgive me, that I hadn't had a choice in keeping her secret . . .

'But secrets aren't as simple as paintings,' he went on. 'I still think if you'd told me what she was going through, we might have been able to save her from that accident. I wonder every time I look at the scar on her face.'

I thought I felt my heart snap. It was hopeless. Every time he looked at Sally, he hated me. I *knew* he'd already decided not to listen – why had he come to me, after all this time, to make me go through this?

'Exactly!' I cried out. I jumped up, full of turmoil. Why couldn't he just let my guilt be enough without his blame too? Why couldn't he trust Sally's judgement and forgive me? He'd confirmed exactly what I'd been afraid his opinion of me was.

'I could apologise every day of my life, Jake, and you'd never be able to forgive me, because we'll never know what would have happened.' I loved him so much. It hurt to stand there so close to him, but so full of frustrated anger. 'You made it clear enough to me in your email, Jake, even if you didn't realise it yourself, that you'd never be ready to listen to me. I don't know why you had to put me through this, on top of everything.'

I turned to storm off but Jake came after me. He grabbed my arm and I flinched, letting out a little scream before I could stop it. I was surprised at my own reaction, and then I realised I was remembering the last time he'd grabbed my arm like that . . . the night of the crash.

If I'd been honest with myself before, I'd have known it already, but that was the moment I realised it was truly over. I was scared of Jake, or at least I was scared of his anger at me. I saw in that second that he would always be holding on to it, and in the same instant I saw our love dying, like I was holding it in my arms, trying to keep it alive but watching it slip away. We were broken.

'Sorry . . . ' Jake bowed his head. He did remember, as clearly as I did. Tears were running down my face because I knew there was no use any more.

'I knew even before your email, the night of the accident. You pointed all your rage and pain at me, and you really hurt me. Physically and the rest. You terrified me. And I know it was a horrible moment for you, I do, but I was going through it too. I love Sally too.'

'I am sorry for that Erica, really. And I know you love Sally.' He sat back down and I thought he might cry too as he held his head. 'But you're right, I guess we'll never know how things might have been.'

We sat there in silence for a long time, or at least it felt like a long time, until Jake's phone beeped. It was the loudest beep, and hearing it was like waking up to an alarm in the middle of an intense dream. He reached into his pocket and flipped open his phone.

'It's Rich, I'm supposed to be meeting him in The Fox for a leaving drink.'

I stood up, feeling shaken and exhausted. And before he could feel like he ought to ask me along I said, 'Well, I'd better get that milk before the shop shuts.'

I pulled at the bottom of my vest top, straightening myself. Was that it? Were we just going to shake hands as if we'd stopped for a chat about the weather?

Jake stood too and we looked at each other. Then he reached out gently with his right hand, still holding his mobile phone, and hooked his two free fingers around my thumb and into my palm.

'I'll miss you, Erica,' he said softly.

'Me too,' I whispered. For a moment, we were back on our bench, discovering our feelings for the first time, kissing, full of joy at discovering each other. We were turning slowly on that roundabout again, leaning on each other in near darkness that Bonfire Night, fingers intertwined like they were designed to be parts of one whole, loving each other, holding on to each other so tightly, believing we'd never let go. Then it was over.

He turned and walked away and I watched, lost and exhausted like I'd been trampled and beaten and with a deep, debilitating pain in my chest. I still loved him, and I knew that he still loved me. But our love was damaged beyond repair.

I turned away too, then, and walked home alone.

Also available in the CosmoGIRL!/Piccadilly
Love Stories Collection

Tessa In Love
Kate le Vann

Tessa has always been 'the quiet one', while her best
friend, Matty, is outgoing and constantly has boys
flocking around her. But Tessa finds a soulmate in
Wolfie, a committed green activist, and she grows
more confident and outspoken every day. She also
begins to look at the world differently . . .

". . . had me living with the characters, laughing
with them, changing the world with them, and if I
dare admit it, crying with them. A fabulous story
– I couldn't put it down."
Wendy Cooling
Reviewer and children's books consultant

ISBN: 978 1 85340 836 6

Loving Danny
Hilary Freeman

Naomi is restless. She's on her gap year and stuck at home with her parents while all her friends are travelling or away at university. Then she meets Danny, a mysterious and intense musician who opens her eyes to a whole new world around her. Danny is exciting and talented, and his band are on the brink of stardom. But he also has a dark, destructive side . . .

Will Naomi be able to save Danny before it's too late? And, more importantly, can she save herself?

"Capturing perfectly the complexities and emotional rawness of first love . . . Warm and witty, compelling and insightful, it's a great read."
Sunday Express

ISBN: 978 1 85340 867 0

Ibiza Summer
Anna-Louise Weatherley

Sixteen-year-old Izzy is on holiday in Ibiza with her glamorous older sister, Ellie, and Ellie's equally gorgeous friends. When she attracts the attention of gorgeous DJ Rex, Izzy is flattered and pretends to be older than she is. But as their relationship deepens, her lies make life more difficult than she ever imagined. Will the truth strengthen their love, or tear it apart?

"An ideal holiday read."
Mizz

ISBN: 978 1 85340 868 7

Things I Know About Love
Kate le Vann

Livia's experience of love has been disappointing,
to say the least. But all that is about to change.
After years of illness, she's off to spend the
summer with her brother in America. She's
making up for lost time, and she's writing it all
down in her private blog. America is everything
she'd dreamed of – and then she meets Adam.
Can Livia put the past behind her and risk falling
in love again?

"Compelling and compassionate . . ."
Carousel

"A rawly honest narrative rich in humour, exposing
the stark realities of a first true love . . .
genuinely moving"
Books for Keeps

ISBN: 978 1 85340 874 8

Boy

...eatherley

... ...es, swimming pools . . .
... ...oks like something out
... y Jones (aka JJ) is a
... ruffy London council
... these two together?

... rashing down when her
... and she moves with her
... r to a run-down house
... . When she's bullied, JJ
... and the two strike up an
unlikely friendship and fall in love.

When a crisis occurs, their differing backgrounds
threaten to split them apart. Against all odds, can
their love survive?

ISBN: 978 1 85340 912 7